FILLOS:

ANCESTRY OF SORCERY

Book II

By Theresa Pocock

FILLOS

Big World Network Publishing

Cover image © 2019 owned by 123RF purchased by Theresa Pocock

Text © 2019 Theresa Pocock

ISBN# 978-0-578-57237-6

Cover Art designed by Theresa Pocock

Managing Editor: Ahnasariah Larsen

Series Editor: Wendy Herman

For all my Tudor-loving peeps. If you are like me, this book is wish

fulfillment. Even the virgin queen deserves romance and a little magic.

#IheartRobertDudly

#ElizabethandRobertforever

#ElizabethTudorSorceress

FILLOS:

ANCESTRY OF SORCERY

Book II

TABLE OF CONTENTS

PART I:
SELF-DISCOVERY

PART II: THE FALL

PART I:
SELF-DISCOVERY

October 1549
Hatfield House, Hertfordshire

All my life I have waited. Everything has its time, its place, and
its season. I waited on my father to love me again, to see me
for who I am, to honor me with his name. I've waited on my
gift to tell me all the secrets I must know. I've waited on Kat to understand I will never love Chaucer and to just let it go. The very nature of
a woman's life is waiting. For men to come home from war, for the servants to light the fire or bring the tea, for the post to come or the day to
end so corsets can be removed. Life is waiting.

But the months following Robert's departure were the hardest waiting I had ever done.

Though strictly speaking, my lovely Robert had not said the words,
"Will you marry me?" For that wasn't the proper order. And he hadn't
said, "I love you, Elizabeth," though I felt like his actions had been telling me those words for years. He also had not promised himself to me,
though in his eyes, I saw a promise.

He had said the waiting would be over. He had said that, when he
came back, the words would be said. I was ready. I had steeled my mind
to it. I would not let anything restrict me from bravely declaring myself,
after he declared himself, as was only proper. I would follow with all the

passion in my soul.

Still, there was waiting.

I knew that as soon as he returned, he would need to go to the council and ask for my hand. That was the correct order of things, and with the Thomas Seymour affair still fresh, propriety would be very necessary. Still, I was so very impatient to be his wife that it distracted me at every opportunity. Like when my current tutor, Dr. Ascham, mentioned dancing lessons, it made my thoughts dance away with Robert in my arms. Or when Kat (my companion, governess, and in many senses, the only mother I have known: Katherine Champernowne Ashley) began speaking of needing more honey in her tea, and there, in my mind, I sat with Robert, the image of him sticking spoonful after spoonful of honey into his own cup.

The only thing that brought solace to my anxious heart was that Kat and Master Parry were returned to me. Lady Tyrwhitt and I had come to a sort of agreement – even, I dare say, a mutual respect. Still, she was my captor in every applicable sense of the word, and my punisher. Edward, my brother and King, sent her in the days following the Thomas Seymour scandal, to make sure I gave the line of propriety a huge berth. So despite our agreement, I was glad to be rid of her when Kat was back to take her place as lead companion in my life. It had almost been a year since I had seen my beloved Kat, and when she was at long last in front of me, I wept so long, it was quite embarrassing.

She wept also and apologized profusely for how she had succumbed to the questioners. But I could not fault her, for it was obvious in her face and in her eyes that the months in the tower had changed her. It took only moments with her to know this was all my fault. I felt it my duty to tell her as much.

"If only I had not let myself fall under the control of that horrid man! Kat… they never would have taken you but for my mistakes. I need to say this, Kat, I must, so listen to me. I have learned… nay, I am changed by this. I cannot tell you all that has transpired in my head this last year. Only now I can see all the ways the devil led me down the road of lust; slowly and beguilingly, working with my pride and vanity.

Kat, I will admit this to you alone, but, when I was with Thomas, under his spell, I cared for no one and nothing and it frightened me. Hear my words now my dearest lady, I will never allow myself to fall victim to lust again, Kat. I will not."

In a perplexing display, Kat's mouth smiled but only slightly, her brow wrinkled but with high eyebrows, making her seem somehow pleased and guilty at the same moment. Then she spoke and I understood her expression. "Elizabeth, I will hear no more of this. What is the role of a governess but to care for and protect her charge from the evils of the world, and from men? One year ago, you were but a tender young woman, barely free of youth. It was my responsibility to keep you safe and I failed. I should have watched you more closely. Why did I not put an end to the nonsense I saw when I could have? Lord help me, I shall never know what possessed me to be so foolish."

In my heart I knew what had possessed her…Thomas had. Just as he seduced and manipulated everyone else around him, he had also cast a spell on Kat, and she was helplessly in his power. I then thought of all the other young women who had fallen victim to his wildish ways, including dear Katherine. The combination of his looks, his way of speaking, his manly will, his power, all combined in a kind of sorcery of his own.

I did not want to feel smug, but I did acknowledge privately that, in the end, I had bested him. I was more powerful than he, and I finally made him taste of the same draft of manipulation and seduction he had spread about so freely. In the corner of my mind that tallied up the battle of will that raged between us, our unfulfilled desires, and the aftermath, I found I had to consider him defeated. Further, I felt vindicated by this understanding, for I knew, with the defeat of such an opponent, I could defeat anyone. Thus the layers of my knowledge, of self and of men, of the very life experience gained from this one situation, were so varied and so numerous, that I knew I would always consider the Thomas Seymour debacle a foundational part of my growth from youth to womanhood.

I still felt a sting though, for I knew Thomas, as so many before him, had paid for his folly with his life. Death was a part of life, I was well acquainted with it, but I had never been responsible. My spirit squirmed and I knew that if I did not shut guilt away, I might never recover completely. And recover I must, for monarchs were forever asking people to die for them, and though I had never admitted it out loud, in my gut, I knew this would not be the last blood on my hands. Yet, it would always be the first.

Squaring my shoulders, I insisted, "Kat, please let us put this behind us. We are both desperately sorry and have learned from our folly. Can we leave it at that?"

My friend dried her eyes and nodded.

"Good," I pulled a false haughty attitude around me like a fine-spun cloak, "for that is a very dreary topic. Now, please tell me all you have done and where you have been."

This was not an end to mine or Kat's sorrow and guilt, unfortunately, though hers was on display a bit more openly. I noticed her random quiet bouts of crying, the dark circles under her eyes, and her downcast expression.

Still, after that first conversation, our friendship was renewed, and we spent the next several days learning to be with one another again and rekindling the very strong bond we had always enjoyed. Kat was more frail than before; I'd heard the tower was hard on the soul, and I took great care with her, fetching and carrying for her, and we rode often, for I knew it was a balm to a heavy heart.

Her condition did do one thing. It distracted my mind from Robert. Guilt was my daily draft now, and a part of me felt grateful for the reminder. Kat and —once the post arrived— Lady Tyrwhitt's daily, spurnful comments on my miserable social status kept my mind quite occupied.

When a few weeks later we received news that the rebellion was over, and that the king and his men had conquered the usurpers, I again felt that burning for Robert in my mind and heart. I had not received a single letter from him while he was in battle, which vexed me greatly. Every day that passed with no letter from him caused me to curse his name and vow to someday return this torture one-hundred-fold, but with the end of the rebellion, word was arriving every day from friends that had been there and those who were close by. My mind was awash with information, though none mentioned my love.

Thus, each day that passed felt like a torment.

Several weeks passed, and the height of my worry seemed to have no bounds. When I was alone in my room, I could allow myself to wallow. There were such fits of crying and trembles all over my body. It was not surprising that I soon felt ill and listless daily.

One evening, Kat and I sat stitching —it was the only thing that matched my miserable mood— when a sudden fear gripped me so tightly, I felt feverish and short winded. Unable to contain my troubles any longer, I rose, allowing my sewing to hit the floor. "What has happened to him?" My hand balled at my knotted stomach. I knew in that moment something had happened to him. I could feel it all the way to my toes. I began pacing and muttering. "Why have I heard nothing?" I did not acknowledge the tears welling up in my eyes. I only pushed on, my mutters transforming into panicked screeches. "I am half mad with worry and yet he sends no news. Kat, is he dead?"

Kat looked at me with astonishment. "What in heaven's name are you talking of, my lady?"

I had not told Kat of Robert and me. After all that had happened, it seemed better to keep my own council in matters of love. In fact, it began to feel like a life principle: matters of my heart kept close to my heart. I briefly wondered how that would look as an epithet stitched to my pillows. But the distraction did not last, for I loathed stitching, and more, Kat was looking at me in her pointed way.

I had to explicate. "I am speaking of my friend, Robert Dudley." I paced as I spoke. "He was here before you came back. He left to fight the rebels and I have not heard if he lived through the ordeal or not. It makes me irrational to think that a friend could be dead, and me, here, sewing, uncertain of it all." I kicked at my sewing circle.

Kat smiled and went on stitching. "It is in the hands of God, my lady, and we will live with whatever He chooses for our young master Dudley. I am sure he is alright. Calm this passion so you do not give yourself a headache."

I glared at her. When she looked up and saw my disposition, she turned her head and raised her eyebrows at me, challenging me to contradict her. My mind fumbled back and forth, but soon couldn't help acknowledging the truth of her words. I sniffed and plopped back down in my chair, feeling quite like a petulant child. "You are right. There is nothing that can be accomplished by worry. Oh," I moaned again as a child would, "why is it that I cannot stop this frightful clench in my middle? It is like a splinter; it irritates at every moment and only gets worse as the days go on."

Kat laughed and said, "My mother always told me that worry is a woman's first work. I believe that she is right, for are we not the ones left behind to wonder what has happened to our husbands or families? Are we not the ones who learn of the turning tides of the world last, yet are expected to prepare the household for whatever comes? Are we not the spouse who truly loves the children and frets over them constantly? Do we not succor the sick and stay at their side until they are well? Our life is worry and patience, and that is our God-given duty and role. Better to wish you were a man than to wish away worry, for I fear the former is more easily obtained."

Her words had comforted me. I was not alone. All women feared for their men. It was, in fact, a rite of my womanhood. "Yes, Kat. I only wish it were not so."

"I do too, my dear, I do too."

I dreamt that night that Robert was damaged. I saw blood and flesh and heard his screams. I woke so scared, I thought I would never recover. I had to accept it now, the dream and the foreboding together. Robert could be dead.

December 1549
Hatfield House, Hertfordshire

Neither Robert, nor any in his family, wrote to me. It gave me hope, for if he were dead, someone would have told me. The word would be everywhere. Robert was known.

Then we received word that John Dudley —Robert's father— had, in a stealthy coup, taken down the lord protector Edward Seymour—my brother the king's uncle, and the brother to Thomas Seymour. The next news was that the council voted John Dudley into two offices. The combination of which effectively gave him the duties of the former lord protector and the steward of the King's property. His titles were now, Lord President of the Council, and Great Steward of the King's Household. Meaning that John Dudley was as good as king of England in all but actual birth and title.

I could not believe it, for if Robert were to ask the council for my hand with his father at its head, there was no way the answer would be no. For had not the ambitious man always wanted a princess for a daughter-in-law?

After months of burning down to coals, all my hopes and desires were reignited. They burned hotter than ever. Robert.

Lord Dudley invited us to visit Edward at court for Christmas. With the death and disgrace of the Seymour brothers, my poor brother and king had lost two of his few remaining relatives, and I knew I would need to be his Bessy when I saw him next, for he would be sad. Also, I prayed for him, hoping the lord to shower down comfort on him, in the way he always had me.

I thought of Mary. She would also come, and I shocked myself when I realized I was eager to see her as well, for this would be the first we had all been together for upwards of two years. It would be good to have family about during the festive time.

Yet, I could not deny in my heart I also longed for a glimpse or news of Robert at court. I did tell myself that if he were in attendance, he would have some very quick talking to do, especially if he expected me to forgive him for such a long silence. But my heart also told me I would forgive him anything if he were just alive. I was hopeful he lived despite the lack of proof, for I felt that if the Lord Protectorate's son had died in the rebellion, word would have gotten about. Of course, when one had nearly a dozen sons as Lord Dudley did, perhaps losing one did not trouble as much as it ought. I did not know Lord Dudley well enough to ascertain his love, or otherwise, for his children. Still, I hoped.

I watched Anna and Kat pack up our things for the journey, wishing, as one hideous black dress after another went into my chests, that I did not have to go on dressing like a grieving widow. However, Kat insisted that this first visit back to court was crucial to my reputation. I must show myself to be a modest and virtuous young woman. I, of course, agreed with her and told myself that I would not look longingly at the other courtier's fine silks and lace. I knew it for the terrible lie it was, but I hoped that, with practice at the glass, my longing looks would be taken for righteous distain.

One of the hundreds of positives to becoming Robert's wife was I would finally be able to dress normally. This thought pushed a smile onto my lips, until I remembered I had no promise from Robert, except that promises would be made when I saw him next. In turn, that thought sent me to the stables for comfort, and all I found there were more questions. These questions were as tired and worn as carriage divots on a London country road. The repeat of them in my mind infuriated me so much, I found no comfort with my horse, and thus returned to the house only to have my pouting interrupted by a knock at the door.

It produced Master Parry. He held a letter in his hands, and I jumped out of my chair and crossed the room quickly even as he spoke.

"A letter for you, my lady princess, from Lord Dudley."

I halted. "Lord Dudley?"

"Yes, my lady. I have read it already, for it was first addressed to me and it is a good letter inquiring only about your health and your happiness and of course your schooling. He adds some news of his son…"

My heart leapt. "Thank you, Master Parry," I said, interrupting him, and took the letter from his hands as gently as I could. "That will be all." And without waiting for his bow, I turned and unfolded the parchment.

My lady Princess Elizabeth,

I hope that you are healthy and happy. Your brother is most anxious to see you as I am sure you are him. We are enjoying the most splendid…

I skipped over all the unimportant drivel and searched the letter for Robert's name. The letter was surprisingly lengthy but finally, I found it. I supposed I would need to read it more thoroughly later.

My son, Robert, begged that I inform you of his situation since he cannot. In the battle, he was shot in the arm and trampled by a horse. The horse also took several balls, those of which were meant for Robert. Unfortunately, the thing fell for dead on top of Robert, smashing his leg and pinning him in a very bad way. Even though he will be as right as rain in a just a few more months —for he is in excellent hands— he wishes for you not to worry over him, for he thinks of you as a dear sister and would not want to cause you unease.

Scanning the rest, I saw nothing else that mentioned Robert, so I went back and read and reread that paragraph. My poor Robert, this news was not at all comforting. He was hurt, he was damaged, and I was not there to hold his hand and comfort him.

Yet this was news of him, and he was alive and not slighting me. He still loved me, I knew it, and I went to my prayer bench for several hours of quite fervent prayer and contemplation.

December 1549
Hampton Court, London

The hours between one sunrise and the next seemed endless. The weeks felt as if the whole world could shrivel like an old apple and be reborn again as I sat watching. It did not help that my world was cold and frozen, and it felt like a reflection of my emotions.

Kat told me I was dramatic, for the whole autumn had been chilly. But I could not help thinking of Robert, broken and cold in this terrible weather, bundled up in bandages with none he loved at hand. I prayed daily that he was healing and not caught with some fever or disease.

However slowly it passed, pass time did, and soon it was time to set out. Travel to court was slow and arduous and I was half-crazed, half-excited with hope.

With the arrival of the Christmas holiday guests to court came the need for me to play the role of the modest and demure princess. I would need to be convincing, for if those at court saw me as a young, innocent girl, they might judge that I was imposed upon by the famously scandalous Thomas Seymore. I hated the rouse, for I knew my part in the matter, but I was desperate to have my reputation repaired. For Robert could never marry a damaged princess. So, despite the tiresome chore, I hoped my motivation would see me through.

Once among all the lovely dresses and simpering courtiers on the first day of entertainment, I found that they did not want to engage me.

Probably afraid of soiling their good reputation. It alarmed me to the fullest. How could I repair my image if no one spoke to me? I admit, at the beginning, I allowed the solitude of my situation to overwhelm me. I found I missed my one and only true compatriot in times such as these: Robin. This missing led me deeper into solitude. I did not want to laugh or dance. I was not merry. I only sat with my memories.

A few days into the great festivities had not led me to see Edward once. I had reasoned out that all were holding their breath in regard to me, waiting to see what the king would do and how he would act toward his disgraced sister.

Finally, I was summoned. My dear Edward was my dear. He pampered me with sweets and complimented me outrageously on my pious dress and manner. I loved seeing him and once it was done, my whole experience at court shifted. It seemed that everywhere I went, people commended me for my plainness of dress and calmness of temper.

Oh, the difference a king's favor can make, especially for one such as myself.

~

On Christmas day, a great feast was held, and I was to see Edward for only the third time since arriving. I readied myself in my most elegant white dress. Though it was plainly cut, it did give me a virginal appearance, which I would need. My hair was loose and natural, and I did not apply any cosmetics or wear any jewelry but my mother's pearls. The entire court would be joining the party, and I would have them all see me looking every inch the maiden I truly was.

I hoped this would throw all their idle gossip back into their teeth. As un-Christian as it was, the thought gave me a small bit of pleasure. I told myself that I was wicked…but after all I had been through and all I had learned and overcome, I could not mean it.

Mary entered. Every inch of her face was covered in paint, every stitch of her gown shimmered gold, and every bare piece of skin sat bejeweled. She started when she looked at me. "Why are you not ready? It is time to leave."

Lifting my chin, I looked crossways at her beautiful velvets and silks, her large gems and her classically beautiful hair and face. Sniffing, I said, "I will be going as you see me."

Mary's eyebrow rose. "Do you not think you could put aside this attitude for one night? I am so very grateful that you have given yourself to modesty and chastity, heaven only knows where the *other* sentiments have led you, but I believe you have taken it too far. Unless you are planning to play the angel Gabriel in the nativity tonight, you will be completely out of place," she said with a smirk.

"Ah, but if I play Gabriel, what part is left for you, my sister, for are you not the only one of us qualified to play that sainted part?" I said as seriously as I could.

Mary was uncertain how to take my words and wrinkled her forehead even as she feigned a light laugh. I smiled to myself and walked out the door.

The party was lavish, with every courtier in their finest clothes and jewels. It had been some time since the court was allowed such frivolity, and I supposed we all owed the evening to the new 'lord protector,' or whatever he wanted to call himself, Lord Dudley.

As Mary and I entered the hall, Edward rushed to greet us, stating in a loud voice, "And here is my sweet sister temperance. Dearest Elizabeth, I trust you are well this evening? You look like an angel."

He was in a grand mood, it seemed. If he were not only twelve, I would have asked if he had been in the wine. He looked as grand as he sounded, in brocaded velvets and fur-lined linens, all studded with jewels and gold embroidery. His plumed hat sat a little askew and I almost *did* ask if wine had been given the boy king.

"I am well, my brother and king. The question is not my state, but yours. You seem as happy as a piglet in its mire." That caused a great laugh from our surrounding nobles. Edward acted affronted for only a moment, and then, seeing my face and those around us, he began to laugh himself.

"You have always had the best wit among us, sister." Then he turned to Mary. "How lovely you look this evening, my lady. Come, let us see you with all the other painted ladies. We shall have a contest to see which of you is the fairest." With that, Edward led a scarlet-faced Mary away. I made the rounds, and when I had ascertained that I did not see whom I wanted, namely Robert or any of his kin that I might question, I sat in a chair to watch the dancing. I felt the dejection overtake me.

It did not take long for other members of the court to sit next to me and speak. I put on my best show, and when my brother called for me to sing, I was feeling up to the task. After I performed for the room, I felt my spirits lift.

At long last, I had the opportunity to speak with John Dudley, but he had nothing new to say about Robert. This disheartened me, but, as I felt his eyes on me the rest of the night—as if he were spying on me—I had to keep my spirits high. It felt as if he were waiting for me to slip up in some way.

I was asked to play and sing several times throughout the night, and I obliged. Also, I had good conversations with both Edward and Mary, though I heard them arguing about religious matters. They were ever at odds. Edward, under the new guidance of John Dudley, seemed to finally be able to express his religious beliefs the way he wanted. Thus, he sent about a letter declaring the Church of England and its practice the only acceptable in the realm, and he began confiscating Catholic Church property as my father had. He also organized a Common Book of Prayers to be given out, that dictated which practices should be changed. England's faithful protestants obliged him, in a way, and those still clinging to the old ways held Mary as their standard of hope. So, Edward reasoned it was time to make Mary submit to him and proceeded to argue with her about it.

When they first met in the grand hall, he commenced a tirade on how she was traitorously holding mass in her chapel. That sent her away, weeping. It was interesting to watch them joust back and forth, for each day brought a new incident. The next evening Mary came looking every bit the much older sister and princess she was, and announced openly that the king was too young to have any sensible knowledge of religious matters. That sent Edward into fits of rage and he, at one time I thought, might make Mary kneel before him or send her to the tower. The conflict between them escalated throughout the entire holiday season.

Nevertheless, we exchanged superb gifts and sang carols. I spent some of the evening in contemplation of that first Christmas night, and gave thanks to the Lord for the gift of the Savior.

The night ended a happy one, with fantastic entertainment, music, food, dancing and conversation. I tried not to envy every beautiful sparkly thing in the room, but I was not sure I succeeded. All were in a jolly mood and I had a grand time despite my need to stay sober.

As Kat undressed me late that night, a realization hit me. Though I had a wonderful time, and I appreciated the comforts and distraction of court, I longed to be back in the comforts and quiets of Hatfield. With a start, I wondered if the social consequences of exile were turning me into a hermit, or if these accursed plain dresses were beginning to make me a lady fit to wear them.

I could not conceive of such a change in my personality, and for the hundredth time, I cursed Thomas Seymour.

However, when Kat asked me about the night and all I could think to tell her was of golden silks, crushed brocades, sparkling diamonds, gaudy rubies and flattering new styles of hair and hood, I knew I was still myself.

This relieved me greatly.

Once the festivities were over, it seemed the claws of the crown came out. As if they were saving it up through the holiday, so as not to start a Tudor war.

The biggest part of this fight was soon brought to my knowledge, and it explained so much of the arguing I'd heard between my siblings.

Edward and the council had issued a letter to all the bishops stating that there was to be a new prayer book in English. With this, there was less point to the Mass, and the power of Rome in our lives would be lessened, for the everyday literate person could read his own service and do so in his own house, should he choose to. It also meant that Catholic

Mass would soon be done away with, as in, not to be held anymore in the kingdom.

Of course, that sent Mary and half the country —those still loyal to Rome— into an apoplexy.

I stayed out of it. I only wanted to have my bench for praying and, beyond that, I was still searching for the answers my soul needed to the religious questions. Besides, no one was interested in what I thought, for my opinion could never affect the world as Edward's could (or possibly Mary's, should Edward meet an untimely end).

There could be no two people with more different feelings on the subject, and with Lord Dudley behind the king, it seemed that England would be completely separated from Rome in a rather short amount of time.

January 1550
Ashridge House, Hertfordshire

Edward gave me a rather shocking parting *gift*. He made me homeless.

After leaving court and all the contention there, I was forced to stay between Ashridge House and Hundson, where Mary had set herself up, for Edward gave Hatfield to John Dudley. My Hatfield. His new position called for new property and Hatfield had been redone by father, and was well-furnished and strategically located. Regardless, I did not understand why Edward should give it away when it was known that I loved it so. Yes, my life was always balanced on the hairpin of the king's pleasure, but I had always been a wonderful sister and friend to him. This greatly vexed me. More so that I had to stay with Mary.

However, part of me understood Edward was under a great amount of pressure just now, so being a kind sister, I decided to reserve my anger for a later meeting and use my angst to employ Master Parry to fervently inquiring after properties. Though a provision of my father's will said that upon my marriage all my properties would be given back to the crown, and Master Parry cautioned it would be a waste of funds, I was resolved. I could not stay with Mary indefinitely. Fortunately, my social standing was on the rise, thanks to my time at court, so property negotiations could be seen as a normal thing for me to do.

Only when one is in favor with the king can one spend one's money. Otherwise, it is frowned upon.

～

The winter dragged on and on, but Mary kept us moving back and forth between Hundson and Ashridge, which kept us away from court, to my relief. I did not want to chance ruining what little rapport my performance at Christmas had bought me. I could not do anything to harm that. So, I stayed in the country, but I made the most of it. I made it a point to go out in my plain dress among the everyday people. I went to those who did not know me and handed out bread and coins. I touched hands and faces with tenderness and spoke to them all.

Soon I felt the benefit of this practice, not only in my heart, which began to lean toward my honest and hardworking countrymen, but also with my image in the minds of the country courtesans. It projected a virtuous, Christian girl, one who would never give herself to the lusts of men, and that idea spread surprisingly well.

Soon, wherever I went, people called out for me, and I realized that perhaps they felt for me now. Perhaps they saw me as I was and felt closer to me. They forgave me my human moment because I showed that I was more than the sum of my faults. Their outpouring of love and support made me more eager to be generous and to show myself to them.

Another change that occurred, concurrent to my rise in esteem with the public, was that Robert's father began writing me. Because of his position as Lord Protector, and my benefactor in accordance with my father's will and my brother's generosity, we had to stay in regular correspondence.

I made a point of writing him back personally and not giving the take to Master Parry, spending hours at my writing table in an effort to impress Lord Dudley with my wit and knowledge. I spoke of the political and social events facing the council and complimented his and the council's actions.

These correspondences had not been going long when rumors of Robert began flitting around. Lord John Dudley never mentioned Robert to me until Robert arrived at court. My heart raced as quickly as a rabbit when I got word that Robert sought a suit with the king and his privy. The rumors also said that it was a marriage suit he was after.

I felt eyes on me whilst riding through town and knew that all suspected I would soon be betrothed. My servants, and even Kat, looked at me with wondering glances; however, none of them spoke to me of what they suspected.

Time passed even more slowly as I agonized daily over the length of time the decision was taking. There could be no doubt of his worthiness, not with his father in the position he was in. There could be no doubt of Edward's approval, for he loved Robert as a brother.

Still, all I could do was wait.

I made myself sick once again with waiting. I took to staying in my bed many hours after dawn and retiring early. Kat felt my mood and left me to it, comforting me only when I asked her to.

February 1550
Ashridge House, Hertfordshire

L ord William Cecil showed up on my doorstep following a letter
from Edward, expressing his need for my opinion of some matters of state.

"William, I am not certain what you want me to do?" I told my
friend quietly as we walked the gardens of Ashridge. "I was there when
father fought for Boulogne. Many good Englishmen died to secure it;
Edward will not easily give it up. Besides, it is a valued port and a na-
tional treasure. Not to mention a thumb and nose to the French."

The gentleman bowed. "My lady, I would never presume such a
thing. For I agree heartily with all you say, as a good Englishman myself.
I am merely suggesting that the king is completely unwilling to see the
benefit French ransom moneys will be to our treasury. We have an opportunity to bargain with the French before they know we are desperate."

"William, are we desperate then?" The Lord Protector Edward Seymour was very liberal in his spread of money. To war, to buildings, to
opulence, and the people had been paying for it. Still, I felt most of it to
be as it should. Unless England was bankrupt.

Ever the ultimate professional, William's face did not indicate how
much trouble we were in. All he said was, "This war with the French
has taken its toll, for certain. It has been long and gruesome. I believe,
and Sir Dudley agrees with me, that Boulogne is the key. Edward can

save face and tell the public the port was willingly ransomed for peace, and we will get the money to pay our dear soldiers and our bills. We can bargain for so much, for we have the port and an eligible king. We have all the power."

"And no money." I said, understanding exactly what the stakes were now.

"Exactly. We defeat both France and Scotland with a marriage alliance between Mary Stuart and Edward, and we show good faith by ransoming Boulogne."

"I see."

"Lord Dudley is ready to send Lord Russel to France with negotiation power as soon as Edward signs off on it. But he is resistant."

"That is why you called on me first. You knew, with so much pressure on him, my brother would need my guidance."

"His urgent letter did give me that clue." William nodded.

Heavens, Cecil was a sly devil. I needed to most certainly keep my eye on him, but more importantly I needed to keep him on *my* side.

I took a deep breath. "If he seeks my council, I will do my best."

"That is all that I ask," he said with a bow.

E dward did seek my council. In the end, he just wanted my opinion of how father would feel—if he were alive—about the treaty with France. We all knew that Father considered capturing Boulogne his last hurrah.

I wrote to Edward, comforting him that father cared more that England and her people were taken care of. After talking to Cecil, I assumed there would be a fight, but I found out later that Edward had called for Lord Russel not five minutes after reading my letter.

It felt wonderful to have helped. I needed to help more, I decided.

March 1550
Ashridge House, Hertfordshire

It was a dark and cold evening. Kat and I retired to the fire in my antechamber early, Kat with her sewing and I with my book. The crackling of burning logs in the hearth was the only noise as we sat comfortably, me in my shift and robe and my hair loose to my waist. I felt melancholy and ready to be alone for the night, but I waited patiently for Kat to tire.

Suddenly there was a knock at the door. I sat up as Blanche entered with a startled look on her face.

She did not wait for me to address her, only blurted out, "Young Master Dudley is here, my lady princess, and he demands to speak with you, claiming his message of vital importance." And before another word could be spoken a voice that made my heart sing spoke from the hall.

"My lady, are you decently attired? May I come in?" I looked at myself and regretted my dreams of receiving him in beautiful silks. However, I succumbed, for his words frightened me.

"Only a moment, sir. One moment, if you please."

Blanche closed the door and I raced to grab the easiest thing I could find to wear. Kat picked up my corset, but I stopped her. "It is only Robert, I do not need to be completely done up. I fear what he has to tell me,

Kat, for he has more manners that any ten gentlemen. Why would he come to me thus if his news were not dire? Hurry, hurry," I demanded. Kat and Blanche pulled the dress over my head and before five minutes had past, Blanche opened the door for him and let her own self out.

I could not even sigh at his beauty. I could not bring myself to think how my pulse raced and my hands trembled. I only sat in my chair staring at him, soaking the sight of him into me.

His voice was urgent. "Please forgive me all, Lady Katherine. I must beg for a private audience with the princess. I have a great many things to discuss with her, some being secret matters of state which must affect her."

The blood drained from Kat's face and she looked to me. I nodded my head and she swept her skirt aside so that she could move quickly. However, before she opened the door she asked, "Sir, please tell me that nothing horrid has happened. Please reassure me or I will be in a fright until I can know everything."

Robert went to her and it was then that I notice a small limp in his walk. "Forgive me, my lady, I did not mean to frighten you. Be reassured that it is nothing that can...physically harm," he stuttered over the words, "the princess. It only pertains to happenings in court and events that will impact the princess'... future. I am certain that she will tell you all momentarily. However, I fear our discussion could be lengthy, so, will you see that no one bothers us, and, if possible, would you be so kind as to wait in your rooms so that my lady princess will have access to you as soon as our audience has concluded? I know that she will need your...counsel."

"Yes, of course! I will leave you now. My lady, come to me if you need me, no matter the hour." I nodded, and only then noticed that I had stood, and that my fingers dug into the palm of my hand and my limbs trembled.

What was Robert about, bursting in here as if the house were on fire, and then scaring us half out of our minds? The only news he could have was with regard to our engagement. I would have heard of anything else.

I only waited for the door to close behind Kat before I moved toward him, a tad unsteadily, and opened my mouth to speak. No words came. I only stared at him, rememorizing every line of his face, every expression of his person.

He looked much older and more serious than the picture in my mind. Robert had become a man. The war, his injury, the time away, had all moved him that way. I looked at him and knew he had seen terrible things. He might have even done terrible things. Regardless, those things had changed him from a youth to a man, and I found that I had never felt such a strong attraction to him. My belly and insides swirled with it.

After several silent moments of staring at him, I finally noticed a tightness to his mouth and forehead that told me he was in pain, but of what sort, I was uncertain.

He stood in stillness as well, seeming to take me in.

I wanted the words to come from his mouth. I had imagined them every day since he left me and now the bloody man was dillydallying.

I had to say something. Something I hoped would help him say the beautiful words that would make me the happiest woman in the world.

"I have…received… many kindly letters from your father… now that he is in his new position." I paused a moment and then went on in a rush. "He told me that you were shot, and that your leg was crushed. I can see that you are limping a bit. Please tell me truthfully, are you well?"

"Yes." His voice came out in a croak and he coughed and started over. "Yes, my lady. I am as well as could be." His eyebrows furrowed, and he blinked several times rapidly, then said softly, and as if he did not want to say it. "I had some very… attentive…care."

I smiled, "I am glad of it. Tell me those to whom I owe gratitude, and I will see that something is sent to them. Of course, their service is more valuable than I could repay, but something must be done. For are you not my very dearest of friends and most loyal of companions?"

With those words, Robert crumpled. The tightness in his lips was from holding his expression together and now he was disarmed, and I did not understand anything on his lovely face. Fortunately, words of explanation began tumbling out of his mouth.

"Father has a scheme that he will not give up. He is convinced that... oh, Elizabeth." He cried out in despair and walked to my side; and taking me by the arms, his clear blue eyes captured my gaze. Then, he spoke the words that I needed. "I am to be married."

My knees went weak with relief and to my shame I sighed and fell to his chest. "Oh, I am so comforted. I cannot believe it. All of this waiting, I thought I should die with anticipation and now..." I pulled away slightly and looked in to his face, which was grief incarnate, but I ignored it and went on. "They gave us permission... I knew they would as soon as your father..."

He pushed himself away from me and yelled, "you are not listening to me! I...I am to be married!" He had never yelled at me before and I stood there, shocked, still unable to see what he was trying to tell me. He paced up and down the rug and ran his hands through his hair. Every few steps, he paused to look at me. I was sure he was on the edge of tears or about to throw something. It was all very confusing.

He suddenly laughed mirthlessly. "You want to show gratitude to the people who nursed me back to health?" He almost growled the words. "Well, make your letter out to Lady Amy Robsart, for it was she and her family that took care of me." He stopped pacing and looked me in the eyes as he continued, "and it is she whom father has arranged for me to marry."

My mouth opened and closed several times as my mind searched for the words I wanted. My eyes held his, searching for a clue as to what was happening... what he possibly could mean. However, I only continued to gape in astonishment, my mind so befuddled that I was not entirely positive I heard him correctly.

Before long, Robert began pacing again, more words pouring from his mouth. "They are Norfolk gentry. Father wants to strength his connections there. Also, Amy is to inherit all her father's land, so 'we will be taken care of.'" He used a condescending tone to quote his father's words.

It was this change in tone that pulled my mind out of the mire. All he said played back to me in my mind and it came like a flood.

Instantly anger was the source that beat my heart and filled my lungs with breath. "Amy!" I growled, "you call her *Amy* and in my presence. As if she were someone dear... someone loved!"

He stopped pacing and looked at me with anguish in his entire countenance. "I told father that I would marry you. Yet he refused me. I told him I would have no other, but he laughed and said I would do as I was told. I threatened, pled, yelled, cajoled, all to no avail. He has said that the point of having children is to marry them off in the best way possible."

This was too much, my anger too overwhelming. So, I shouted. "And what of marriage to a Princess? Is that not the best there is?"

"He does not need to strengthen the bonds to the Tudor line. He is Lord Chancellor. And he and the king have other plans for you."

"HE... he has other plans for *my* marriage. Who does he think he is?"

"He is what he is, Elizabeth, you know as well as I. Elizabeth..."

"Do not name me thus, Sir! I am your princess." I raised my chin as I whispered wrath at him.

Deep sorrow tainted his angry features, yet he spoke quietly, "pardon me, my lady princess." He took a step toward me, his palms raised to me as he spoke. "I stayed at court so long to remind him that he had set us together himself. Of course, it was only to try and play to his ego, but he would not listen. I begged him to reconsider and told him in detail how we... how I felt. Eliza... my lady princess, he threatens to send me to the gallows if I disobey him." He paused and took another step toward me. "I came here to beg you to advise me. What shall we do? What can we do? For this feels like life or death to me."

I said nothing as I let the anger burn me up, so that his eyes would not douse the flames and all of me turn to ash. When my silence continued, he went on with yet another step toward me. "I would rather die. Believe me, if I would have known how it would be when I returned from war, I would have stayed beneath that horse and let my life seep away with the blood that drained from my wounds. Yet your eyes came to me, your scent swept over me with a breeze from God, and your re-membered touch bolstered me. You are the one that saved me, not Am... not this other." His eyes were winning the battle and I felt my anger slip. "I do not know what my father plans, however I do know that aside from fleeing England or death, I can see no way out of this."

Suddenly I seethed again. I swept away from him, whispering in a voice as cold as death; "How dare he! How dare both of you! How is this possible? I have no words for this... this vile betrayal... this treason to my person, to my heart. It is everything that I have always feared from love. It is what happened to my mother all over again. It is shameful and honorless. It is my worst nightmare come to pass and it is at your feet, Robert, all of it. It is by your hand and at your feet." Robert reached for me, horror in his eyes at my words, but I moved as far away from him as I could. "Don't you touch me. Don't you come near me."

He pleaded, "please, let us talk this through. There must be some..."

"I think we have done quite enough talking. Get out of my sight, Robert Dudley. I never want to see you again!" My voice rose with every word and, because I was standing right next to the door, I opened it for him and pointed as I gritted my teeth and whispered, "out."

He stood there, beautiful in his sadness and anger, but I would not think of his beauty ever again. He would never be mine now, he would be hers, and there was nothing I could do about it.

"I will not leave until you tell me that you *will* see me again, so we can discuss this." His eyes would not look away from mine.

"I will never see you again," I said to him as devoid of feeling as I could. "Now leave me." However, my voice betrayed me with an emo-tional crack and the moment it did this, he began marching across the room toward me. When he got to me, he wrenched the door out of my hand and slammed it shut.

With one twist of his body, I was roughly pushed against the door, and Robert had my face in his hands. He was fuming and miserable and I could tell, as he clutched my face so urgently, that I was not going to get out of this unscathed.

I had no will to fight him off, for he looked into my eyes with a longing I had seen before, but only in a few precious, private moments. His breath heaved through his flared nostrils and soon, his eyes moved from my eyes to my cheeks. His thumbs pressed against the bones there, and when both his thumb and his eyes traveled to my lips, I knew that here and now, we would share our first and last kiss.

I instantly did not want it to happen. I did not want to finally taste the most delicious fruit in all the world and then watch that fruit be given to another, never again to be tasted by me. However, before I could act, Robert had slid his hand from my face, around to the back of my neck and, with a momentary glance back up at my eyes, he crushed his lips into mine.

His mouth opened and closed around my trembling, eager lips and I thrilled at the sound of our joining as they blended and moved together. I melted at the feel of his soft full mouth, his warm hands cradling my face.

For the first time in almost a year, I drank in his sweet smell as it overwhelmed all other scents. At first, he devoured me, but I only had time to taste him and smell him and admire him before the kiss had calmed. Robert kept me captured, but he reluctantly pulled his mouth from mine, though he kept our foreheads together.

I opened my eyes and pushed gently on his chest, needing to see him. He backed away barely an inch, his cornflower blue eyes bright in the firelight. I saw that wet tears clung to his beautiful black lashes and more ran down his face. His beautiful mouth turned down in the saddest of expressions.

Then a small huff of misery came from his throat and, in that moment, I was overwhelmed with a feeling of loss. Such brokenness, such heartache... I could no longer control myself either. Tears flooded my eyes and spilled down my cheeks as I tangled my fingers fiercely in Robert's thick hair and smashed my body and lips against his in an even tighter, more passionate embrace. His breath was heavy, he sniffed and groaned sadly. His limbs moved; an arm tightened about my waist and his hand grasped at the hair at the back of my neck almost violently.

We did not stop the desire that drove us to touch. My fingers traveled every inch of his face, as we breathed and kissed and loved. His hands caressed my shoulders, my back, my arm, my hair. But our lips stayed close. Our eyes only needed intermittent gazes. I breathed his air and he mine, and we mingled our tears and our mouths and our grief.

I never wanted this to end. He would never have enough of me and I knew I would never be done with him, But at exactly the right moment, our breathing quickened. Our kissing became less urgent, less about taking our heartache and anger out on one another, and more about passion for the other person. I felt changes in my own body first. It brought my mind to forbidden things, and I lingered over these thoughts as I began to stop all movement but that between our lips. I deepened our kiss and Robert was the first to experiment with involving more than just our lips.

This sent a very different sensation through me, and it grew very quickly and very strong as our mouths mingled in a different way. Just as this feeling became uncomfortably vast, Robert swept me off my feet, our mouths untangling for a few moments. He maneuvered us around my antechamber, and I felt a scary thrill as he moved us into my inner room. He carried me to my bed and laid me down where he held himself over me and again kissed me with fervor.

Slowly, he lowered himself down to me and I knew I had to make a very important choice. The weight of him felt so perfect. I pulled his shirt out of his breeches, needed to touch him. My hands went up the skin of his back and his mouth pulled away from mine as he moaned. Our eyes met, and I saw that he was having the same frightening desires as myself.

There was a choice to be made here. One that could never be undone or taken back. Robert bit his lip as he reached into my soul with his breathtakingly beautiful eyes. Every part of me wanted him and I could see that every part of him felt similarly.

Still, he forced himself to move off me. He lay at my side up on his elbow, holding himself up so he could look at me. I intertwined our legs as I curled toward him, pressing my chest against his. We breathed together for a moment. Then Robert reached his hand between us and took my chin. He pulled my eyes up to his and he began caressing my face. His eyes were brimming with tears once more, his countenance calmed and somber.

Suddenly he said, "I love you Elizabeth. I love you so much that it does me injury to be away from you. I have felt keenly the distance between us these past months. You cannot know what I have suffered." He took in a quick breath and brushed my hair back. "Every part of my soul is yours. I have no idea how I am going to...." He choked and looked away from me. "How will I ever be able to..." he whispered, then stopped completely, unable to finish, his face crumpled in pain. In the expression, I saw the boy I'd known for half my life. The boy I'd loved as long as I could remember loving anyone. In his face, I felt my own pain.

A moment later, he said more clearly, and with a very small smile, "I have loved you from our first moments by the lake at Hatfield so long ago." He paused again, and I saw in my mind the same memories he thought of. "Of course, that love was a drop compared to the ocean that rages inside me now." Then his face became solemn and intense and he whispered, "this body was *made* for you to love." He pounded on his chest. "This soul was made to be your companion forever." He pounded on himself again. "We are supposed to be for one another alone and not for anyone else. Elizabeth, I want to have this with you. I want us to be connected in a way no one can take away. I want us to man and wife in all the ways it matters. You are first. You are my first. Please, let me make love to you, for it is the way we were meant to experience first love, true love. I do not want this with anyone else." He bit his lip to stop its quivering and brushed my cheek tenderly.

His words were perfect, they were everything I wanted to hear, and everything I wanted to do. Torn between what I should do and what I wanted more than life or breath, I pulled him close and said the only words I could say that would tell him I had to refuse him, though I did not want to. "You are the only man I could ever marry or ever love. I swear to you now that this body will only ever be yours. This soul will only ever be *your* companion. I choose you. I choose a life with you or a life with none. I will *love* only you with all of me no matter what the future holds, I promise you this." And I kissed his cheek. His salty tears clung to my lips, burning them.

My words lit a fire in his eyes. "I had already made that same promise to you in my heart. I only waited for the proper and natural time to say the words. Now, I am forced to break a promise that has already become a part of me, a promise I am already wholly committed to. How can I do what I must? Why can it not be different? Elizabeth, I have asked you to be my wife a thousand times in my heart, why cannot the wishes of my heart come true, why am I a slave to other people? We both are slaves to others." Angry tears were pouring down his cheeks and his voice had risen with the passion he felt.

Robert was not an emotional man, and it hurt me so much to see him broken this way. I knew exactly how he felt, for he was speaking and acting out my own soul's words and desires. In this moment of consideration, I realized a truth. There was a third option here. It was hard and very dangerous. But I saw it and it lived outside the normal, accepted way of things. It went against my upbringing.

I saw a promise between two people. A promise they could keep to one another. And I saw myself constructing a life around that promise. Then I realized I had already said my promise to him. I had already given him my vow.

Acting against all decorum, against all tradition and yes, perhaps even against God's commandments themselves, I knew what I had to do. I knew what was right for us.

I pulled his damp face down to mine and gently kissed his perfect lips and I saw something further. This was how we were meant to experience first love, together... Robert and Elizabeth. The experience might haunt us both, but Robert was right. This was meant for us.

"Say your vows to me husband, for I have already said mine to you."

His eyes lit. He sniffed and regarded me. I blinked at him and smiled. I saw as he understood my full meaning. He wiped at his face after a moment of thought, reached into his jacket pocket. He pulled out a small piece of ribbon. It was a very abused off-white and thread bare. I glanced at him, questioningly. He sniffed once more and took my hand.

"I have carried this ribbon with me for eight years. It's yours. I found it near the water that first day we played in the pond. And I took it. Do you remember?"

I smiled and nodded. "So that is why it is so tattered. Have you never washed it out?"

"No, it is tattered because it has been through many things with me. It has, for the last eight years, been on my person every moment of every day, just as you have been in my heart every moment of every day." Robert sat up, bent down to his boot, pulled out a knife, and with a quick motion severed the ribbon in two. "I will get you a ring one day, but for now…" He tenderly placed one half back in his pocket and gathered up my hand again. As he spoke, he wound the ribbon around my marriage finger and tied it with a deft knot. "Just as I have been faithful to my representation of you for the last eight years, my heart will be faithful for the next eighty. With this ribbon, I give you my oath. I will love you always. You are the wife of my heart. You are the mate of my soul. My mind will never betray you; my heart will never forsake you. I am yours. Forever. You and I are bound by the true love we have, and it is as unbreakable a binding as any god could bless, because we choose it. Despite what we are forced into, all we must face in the future, we choose each other. Elizabeth, this is my promise before you and God. I will choose you for as long as I live."

My heart raced inside my chest. Robert's vow was the most beautiful thing I'd ever heard. I looked at the ribbon around my finger and felt to my bones that he was my husband in all the ways that were important. I knew that what happened next would be difficult, but his promise gave me such hope.

And this, right now, was the only chance I would ever get to have him completely for myself. *Amy* could not have this… no one could, because this was destined for me.

I lay next to him in my bed with the sun barely peeking through a small gap in the drapes. Rolling over, I smiled to myself as I gazed at Robert's untidy hair and sleep relaxed face. He was the most beautiful man in the world and in my mind's eye, I watched him in all his beauty above me, in the depth of sweaty passion and instantly, I wanted him again.

Stifling a giggle, I brushed his nicely shaped back with my hand and snuggled in closer to his side, yet he did not move. He must really be tired, for all it had taken a few hours ago was a look, and he was kissing me.

It was then that I heard someone come through the door of my antechamber. Quickly I grabbed my nightdress and pulled it on as I tried to rouse Robert. His eyes finally fluttered open and I took his face in my hands. "Be as silent and as still as the dead." He blinked in confusion as I threw my many pillows atop him and piled the blankets up haphazardly, just as a knock sounded. Snuggling myself under the blankets, I moaned, "come." I was going to feign sickness.

Kat stepped in and pulled back the curtain a bit. Anxiety wrinkled her brow. Thankfully, she did not even look around the room, for I only now recalled that I had not hidden Robert's clothes. Luckily, she only had eyes for me. "I have just heard about Robert. I did not know you had your heart so set on him. Oh, my dear girl." She rushed to my side and knelt by my face, taking my hands in hers. "Have you been up all night crying? I am so dreadfully sorry." And she smoothed my hair back and looked into my eyes intently.

In that moment, the situation came crashing down on me even more than the night before, for now I realized how badly I desired to be with Robert forever. I felt it before, but now I *knew* it. Tears instantly flooded my eyes. If only I could take back this night filled with pleasures, I would not have to covet it my whole life long. Why was I such a fool?

The horror and despair I had ignored for the last eight hours began to drown me. I wept bitterly. I wept and wept, not caring that Robert was lying next to me, hearing every sob, feeling every shudder. Kat held me and stroked me until I was done.

Finally, I sniffed, "Kat, thank you so much for being here with me, but would you mind leaving me now? I want to be alone. I have a horrid headache and I did not get any sleep last night. Also, I am afraid you must make excuses for my appointments today, for I fear I will not be able to leave this room."

She stood. "Of course, my lady. Please ring the bell if you need the smallest thing. I will see to it myself." She bent and kissed my forehead and walked to the door. I filled myself with power and prepared to once again use it on Kat, but I did not need to. She did not look back or see Robert's clothes.

I moved to lying on my back and saw, out of the corner of my eye, Robert slowly fold down the blankets and pillows. His hand moved to touch me, but I shuddered away from it. How could I bear it in spite of my desire for it? Listening to my desires had gotten me into such a mire that I felt the possibility of never reemerging, or if I did, I would be changed, wounded, hobbled.

"My love." His voice held emotion and I realized that he was just as hurt as I. Turning toward him, I found what I knew I would, tear-stained cheeks and eyes filled with sorrow. I moved to him and held him and he me. He cried and kissed every bit of my face repeating, "I love you...I love you...I love you," between kisses. I cried too. We cried together for what seemed like hours. Then I got angry, pounding on him and kicking my legs and screaming into his chest. Finally, I cried a little more while I kissed him fiercely, and then we made love again and again and again... until we could not anymore.

Robert could only stay for a few short weeks, but we made the most of it. Slipping out whenever possible, sneaking away to kiss and talk. He slept every night in my bed, and I hid him if he did not waken in time. I ignored the dread I felt when away from him, and smiled while he was with me, and I knew he was doing the same thing. I manipulated without prejudice anyone who saw us or caught us, and learned how it was not difficult for me to force people to become so confused that they did not know what they saw or heard. This was very convenient and, though Robert could see as I lit up like a candle and see the result as people went away from us blabbering about something completely random, he only ever said something to me once.

"Have you ever done that to me?" He did not act strange as he walked along, holding my hand as if he had just asked me if I had ever seen the sun. "I mean before I knew that something was being done."

"No… never. I swore that I would not the moment I saw some of my earlier follies. Anyhow, it seems you have always been on my side… so there was never a need," I said, and pressed myself against him while I began kissing his neck. He whimpered when I did that and before long, we were running, very clandestinely, through the halls, giggling and playing as we did when we were young.

In those short sweet days, we teased one another and talked like we always had, but with more passion. Kat looked at us disapprovingly, but I told her that if Robert were to be married, I wanted to have all the old experiences with him one last time. And so, she let us galivant around as if we were children. Of course, in private, our interaction had a flirting playfulness that was inappropriate for unmarried people, but as the days went by, I felt more and more married to the love of my life and less and less guilty.

On the evening before Robert was to leave, I changed into my riding dress and went down to the stable. Robert only had Bessy out and he stood looking out the back stable door toward the setting sun. His hat was discarded, his coat and the laces of his white shirt undone. I was so overwhelmed by how magnificent he looked, his fine form still and comfortable as the sun shone around him, illuminating him as if *he* had an aura of light. His brown hair sparkled with the little touches of the red it held, and his curls aligned perfectly on the back of his head. Bessy's reins were in his hand as he gently patted her.

My tears could not be controlled. They flowed, betraying all the sorrow I had hidden from him, and from myself for the past week. He turned and saw me and, without a pause, came and held me.

I heard Henry whistling as he always did while about his work, and I pushed Robert away, as he whispered in my ear, "I thought we could *both* ride Bessy. I cannot stand being a horse's width away from you, not today, in truth, not any day."

The tears came faster, and I said, "yes, but let's be gone before Henry finds us."

Robert helped me up and, in a moment, we were out of the doors and leaving the world behind.

Robert let me have the reins and held me around the waist so tight that I could feel every inch of him pressing against me. Occasionally, he would kiss my neck and whisper, "I love you forever," in my ear. I could not talk. All I could do was ride and weep, and I knew that he was weeping too.

Dust gradually cooled the sky, but I could not care. It matched the mood that surrounded us. The world took on an ethereal feel, and with the energy of the last rays of light zipping around us, it was as if we could overcome everything. It felt as if, despite it all, we *could* be together. What was between us would transcend time and distance and other relationships.

I pulled Bessie to a halt at the ridge of a hill covered with skeletal oaks, and then carefully maneuvered myself around on the horse so that I was facing him. I pulled the blanket in my arms around us to keep my exposed legs warm after I wrapped them around him. He took up the reins and maneuvered the horse as I wiggled around getting comfortable. In truth it was not comfortable, but it was what I wanted.

Once I was settled, Robert and I were nose to nose. I looked into his eyes and willed him to know how much I loved him and needed him.

Soon, he interrupted the silence. "Elizabeth, just speak the words and I will forsake everything, home, family, pride… and I will run with you…far away from here. To the mainland, if need be, and we will buy a little farm and raise a family. Ask me to do this, tell me it is what you want and let the rest of the world be damned. We will be poor, and treasonous traitors, but we will be together. We can live out our days in peace. That is all I want."

I looked up from his chest and rubbed my hands up his arms to his face. "That is what I want more than anything… but… but there is something that I have not told you."

He cocked his head to the side and narrowed his eyes uncertainly. "Oh? What is it?"

I straightened my blanket to cover me up a little more and began to speak. "We have not talked about my… gift." My cheeks flamed, and

I turned my face away from him. Though I wanted to tell Robert every-thing, there was still that thing in my heart that needed me to hold back. Still, I pushed myself forward. "I will tell you all, husband of my heart. I promise. But for now, let this suffice: I believe there is a reason God has given me the gift he has. I believe that he will one day put me in a position to make a difference in the world." My heart raced as I said the words out loud. Admitting *this* felt far more exposing than anything I had ever said.

Robert thought for a moment then said, "you think that God intends the crown of England for you."

"I do not know!" I wailed and buried my face into his chest. "Per-haps I am meant to be a very influential member of court, or a musician or theologian, I haven't a clue. However, I do know that I am the first *fillos* in the history of my ancestors that has the potential to reign."

"Fillos?"

"It is what my family calls our power," I stated quickly, wanting to move on.

"Wait, what? Your family?"

"Many members of my female line have had the same gift."

Robert's blue eyes were wide with surprise.

I went on, "my mother began the battle for the crown, and she hoped that I would finish it. Why do you think I study so hard or spend so much time at my prayer bench? Why do I inform myself in every political and social movement? Not only because I love to learn, and I feel God has given me a mind that is built for learning, but because I am preparing myself and seeking to find out what God would have me do. It is what my mother wanted for me. In truth, it is why she did everything she did. I feel tied to this mission, as it were with cords of metal, and though I want to have you more than anything, I am *part* of this quest... it *is* me, I could no sooner cut off my own hand."

He studied my face and breathed heavily as he contemplated the gravity of my words. However, a moment later, he smoothed his expres-sion and took my chin in his free hand. "I understand, my love. There will be no running away. It was just a fancy that took me. Forgive me. I suppose I too have obligations that I cannot forsake." Just the mention of that subject, and there was tension in his forehead and sadness in his eyes, and my own body raged with clashing emotions.

We looked at one another, both sad, both angry, both hurt. Suddenly, he pulled my lips to him and kissed me fiercely, a kiss that said goodbye. And then, abruptly, I knew... he was saying goodbye... goodbye to hope, to escape. When he was finished, he continued to hold my face in his hands, stroking my cheek; and suddenly he laughed, which made Bessy prance a little.

When he settled her down, I asked, "why, pray tell, are you laughing at me, good sir?"

Wiping the smile off his face, he said in a serious tone, as he settled the horse underneath us down, "I don't know... it is just you. You are so...amazing. God only calls a few to do his work, and those he calls must give more than the rest of us. I suppose I am just grateful that I will at least be around to watch you... to see the work you do. To see what you become. It is inspiring to see how he will use you to do good. Who among us gets to see God's hand?"

I loved his faith in me. He had nary a doubt that I would forsake what I wanted to do for what I felt the Lord wanted me to do.

This man was not made of the same material as other men. He was superior to them in every way and I did not believe it was breeding. It was who he was. He was a man of faith who cared more about his loved ones than himself. His words of kindness, and his complete and genuine acceptance of my call and its ramifications, took my breath away.

His beauty by moonlight, but also his beauty of heart and soul, set my body afire. I had had enough talk. I only had one thought besides the feel of his lips as I kissed him goodbye.

Tomorrow, Amy Robsart will be the luckiest woman in the world, but for tonight, I am.

June 4, 1550
Hampton Court, London

I knew that Robert was my husband. I had given myself to him and I would be faithful to him, but I did not know how this arrangement would work. If I had wanted to discuss it, I know Robert would have done so with me, but it was too painful. I just decided that I would ignore it and keep my vows to him. I was not with child, so that was fortunate. I had no idea what I would have done if that had happened.

There was only one point of certainty in my life in this moment, and that was: I would look more beautiful at Robert's wedding than the bride. I had Kat and Blanche working on me several hours before the wedding was to take place. As Kat cinched the laces of my corset, I groaned with discomfort. "Not so tight, Kat. I cannot breathe."

"I do not understand why you are suddenly so sensitive about your corsets, my lady."

"I just hate it; it is not a new thing for women to hate the accursed thing." I breathed out as she pulled. "Perhaps they need to be refitted."

"I have noticed a rather shocking amount of bosom at your neckline. You surprise us all and have bloomed *late* in this *one* area."

"Yes, a sixteen-year-old princess finally getting her bosoms, what will the world say?" Blanche cackled in the naughty way she did.

Kat blushed. "I will have the seamstresses up tomorrow."

I glanced down at the bosom in question. I was forming up rather nicely and Robert had not seen me in months, which meant he did not know of this new development. A little thrill of triumph wiggled up my spine.

"Well, my lady princess, you are a vision." Blanche stated, once again serious.

I turned to look in the glass. I saw the image of a fair-skinned woman with a high forehead, a heart-shaped face with radiantly flushed cheeks, a narrow--but not quite plump--mouth and wide, innocent eyes of black. She was tall and thin and wearing the first decent dress in years: layers upon layers of white and gold satin skirts, with a pearl encrusted bodice and sleeves. Her red hair was held back with a small golden caul, and a circlet of spun gold with pearl inlays crowned her head.

Perfect. Absolutely perfect.

Fingering my mother's necklace that was of course around my neck, I noticed in the mirror, all of the rings glittering on my fingers. They had sat in a box for the past two years, and I was very happy to have them on.

Satisfied that I could look no better, I turned to face Kat, who said, "you look ravishing, my lady princess." She sniffed. "I hope you are not planning on outshining the bride. That would be unkind."

I raised an eyebrow at her. "I would never dream of doing such a thing. I only must look the princess that I am." I smiled innocently, and Kat shook her head slightly, but said nothing else.

These women were the only in the world who knew of my heartbreak. Kat had spoiled me with days in bed and extra sweets and handkerchiefs to cry into for weeks. I still was not done with all of that, and I feared that I never would be. Even with my gift, I was powerless to change that the only man I could ever love was getting married to someone else today, in front of God and everyone …and after all my hopes.

With the doubts that our marriage of the heart would be erased today with a piece of paper, and no understanding of what my life would be like now, I felt all aflutter with grief and fear. How could I possibly manage this net of terror and heartache I'd woven for myself?

Shaking my head fiercely to push away the mounting tears, I turned again to look in the mirror and prepared myself. I would control what I could.

Edward attended. He actually stood near me, but on a small dais. John Dudley stood at my side, and the fury that enveloped me at the sight of the man was more than I could trust myself with. So, I did not speak to him. Several times, he tried to capture my attention, speaking to me of this or that, but I only acknowledged him with an inclination of my head and then turned away from him.

Finally, the time arrived. The groom was dressed finely, yet I saw the tight forehead and mouth, and I knew that he was not happy. Upon entering the hall, he instantly found me, eyes darting from face to face until they saw mine. I smiled as best I could, and he looked on the verge of tears, but gave me a small return smile.

I had never seen Amy Robsart before and I wished I never had. I was not a beauty, though I did have enough charms to suffice. Robert thought me beautiful, which was all that mattered. Amy, on the other hand... *she* was *very* beautiful. Blonde curls framed a round face with wide, innocent eyes shrouded in thick, dark lashes. Her face was so sweet, I almost wept upon seeing her, and she looked so radiant in her simple, yet elegant dress, that I felt almost foolish. I saw how she trembled as she passed me, and I momentarily felt sorry for her. However, I ruthlessly crushed that feeling as she took Robert's hand and the ceremony began.

Robert looked at his bride hesitantly just as the vows started, and I called the light to me. I did not whisper or mouth the words, only said them in my heart. *"You will find happiness with your wife. You will see the good in her and... love her."* I stumbled over the thought of the last few words, and had a very hard time thinking them in truth; but, concentrating hard, I forced myself to make them true. Then, with the sending of the light, I gave Robert the only wedding gift he would get from me: his very first manipulation.

As the light hit him, he turned away from the priest, away from his bride and looked at me. I knew he could see the light surrounding me and I wondered if he felt the manipulation that I just placed upon his mind. As he looked at me, his face flashing quickly through emotions, I knew each one... I knew precisely what he was thinking, feeling. My hand went to my heart as a tear ran down my face and I returned his sentiments with cautiously mouthed words. *"I love you."*

He smiled and turned to look at his bride.

When I returned to my room, there was a small parcel on my side table. Kat noticed it first and brought it to me. "What could this be?" she wondered.

It had my name on it and I recognized the handwriting. Robert. I took it and asked to be left alone. Kat looked at me questioningly but obliged me. I opened up the paper and then the small box inside. What I found surprised me fully. It was a small plain circle of gold with a piece of parchment rolled inside it. My heart began to race as I pulled the scrap out.

My wife,

I promise to love you forever, to support you, to comfort you, to heed your counsel and to stay faithful to only you. I say your name before God today in my heart. I make my vows to you. I promise to be by your side as much as God grants me and to appreciate every breath we breathe together. Please except this band as a sign of my commitment.

Yours,
R

I was on my knees, tears running down my face. I could not be surprised at this statement. Robert was Robert. That he had thought of me in this moment made my heart sing with joy. I ripped all my beautiful rings off my left hand and slipped Robert's gift on the appropriate finger. I did not care what role I would be forced to play in this world, that ring would never be off my finger.

July 1550
Hatfield House, Hertfordshire

R obert wrote to me right away. He told me of where he was, Norfolk. There were still some rebellious pockets of people in the countryside and Robert had been set to secure the area by his father. It was a very friendly letter and it made me crazy. However, I followed suit and wrote him back in the same manner.

By some miracle, Lord Dudley agreed to let me back in my house at Hatfield, temporarily, of course. Perhaps he could tell how vexed I was with him. Perhaps he realized what a terrible mistake he made in keeping Robert and I apart. Perhaps he knew I was not someone to trifle with.

Still the news came a bit too late, for Master Parry and I had made several deposits on other properties. It would not be long until I had to start moving from house to house every month to rest the house and keep from the heat. With all of my newly acquired homes, I used the excuse of touring them to keep myself busy.

I had several dreams about Robert. They left me unsatisfied and worrying about the state we found ourselves in. But one night in particular, I saw Amy in my dreams, with my husband, and I woke fully aware of how it would feel if Robert exercised his husbandly rights on his true wife. And that left me in a state.

I could not concentrate. I was beyond distracted. Would he take her clothes off? Would his lips caress hers? Would he...? My hands ripped at my hair. I wanted to claw out my eyes and scream at the top of my lungs. More, I wanted to race to their home in Norfolk and rip him away from her, tear him out of her arms and drag him into my bed. How could I live this way? How could I ever look at either one of them again knowing what they had done... knowing what she had taken from me. My back arched painfully, and my heart pounded as I struggled. Finally, I stuck my head in my pillow and screamed until I was hoarse, and then I cried until I had shed every last tear my body held. I panted and sweated and finally, I settled down.

In the dark of the night, my mind replayed this dream for weeks. So much so, that I dreaded sleep.

August 1550
Hatfield House, Hertfordshire

The summer was dreadfully hot, and I could do nothing but bake and throw myself in to my schoolwork. Sitting in the schoolroom, translating a portion of the tragedies of Sophocles into French felt so fruitless, unfulfilling.

Between the dreams and missing Robert terribly, and the monotony of my days, I began to consider how I regretted the decision to be with Robert in the carnal way. Robert and I had spoken about the consequences of our unlawful marriage, but in my solitude, it felt as if I were the only one having to pay them. I was the one who had to be alone with my thoughts, memories and desires. I was the one sullied by our love. I was the one who did not get to enjoy those pleasures again for the foreseeable future, and I was the one who had to lie about it if the subject came up. Those thoughts made me wish I could take it back. Not the marriage, just the lovemaking. It was better before I knew.

Also, I felt I could not trust Robert. I had seen him in my dreams making love to Amy. How dreadful it was. How it haunted me. How confused I was by his loving letters. How I longed to ask him about it all. How I regretted it all.

Another consequence, and perhaps the worst one, was that I felt God had abandoned me. My time on the prayer bench was empty. No joy or love crept through my soul as it had done before. I knew that what I had done was a sin in His eyes and I had no justification for it. The emptiness in my heart and soul made me truly appreciate the sacrifice of my Savior, for I had not known how much God was in my life before I had offended him, and the only way to get that loving and necessary relationship back was through Christ's sacrifice. I had done wrong, but Christ could make it right if I would let him. A pang of the doubtful questions burned through me. Would I do it again if I knew I had to trade Robert for a relationship with the Lord? Was it worth it? I did not know yet.

At the time, I had told myself that marrying Robert in my heart was enough justification for fornication. I eyed the band of gold around my finger. It did not feel like fornication. I was committed to him as if he were my lawful husband. He felt the same, but he was weak. A man. I was not so. I was strong. I would never have another. I hoped my dream was wrong. I hoped he would never consummate his marriage with Amy. But I realized now, as the logistics of the situation became reality, that my marriage of the heart to Robert held no weight.

Marriage was made to protect women, not to enslave them. It forced a man to be committed to his mate in the eyes of god, the law and his peers. I had none of that. What if I had been pregnant? A babe within a marriage was a blessing, one outside of it a curse, and not for the sake of piety, but for the sake of the poor woman. I saw the way good men worked and fought for their families. They braved the world so that their wives and children could be safe and comfortable. That male half of the marriage equation was vital, and I respected it and wanted men to provide and protect all women, the world over. But in my marriage to Robert, this very real but very uncertain marriage of the heart, I would never have that either.

In that moment, I realized what a perfect web I had made for myself. How all my fears and insecurities had led me to this spot. I never truly wanted to be married. Perhaps not even to Robert. I did love him, desperately, but I didn't want to be tied down the way other women were, to husband and children. I had never wanted that, not with Thomas, not with Robert. I had put myself in a position where I would never have to do it. I was committed in my heart to a man I loved but could never have. And the only way to make sure I would never be tied down with children was to make sure I never made love to that man again which, considering the consequences, and considering that he probably had that relationship with his true wife, made it an easy choice. Fornication was one thing, but I had already decided adultery was out of the question; that road had been walked before and learned from.

Thus, it all wrapped up quite nicely.

This profound understanding of what I had committed to for my lifestyle made it easier to go to God and ask for forgiveness. I would not be repeating my sins. Still, I heard silence.

I needed to know what God wanted from me, but with his silence, I turned to my other source of knowledge. When school lessons were over, I went straight to my room and collected my mother's journal. I had begun reading it more thoroughly.

Stepping outside, the warmth of the air refreshed me after sitting so long in the schoolroom. I sat under a massive oak and opened to my current page to read. Several things instantly caught my attention for the first time.

I do not know when I will die, but the plague is so horrid through the village that I am sure to get it. Jane is at her aunt's and so she will be safe. However, she is old enough that her training is almost done, and I have but one more thing that I could give her and that is my gift itself. My ability to call down rain has helped our village innumerable times, and I would like Jane to have it since her power is so small. I think I have devised a way to pass it to her, but I need to be with her when it is done, and it must be done freely. I only hope that I will see her before I go.

I flipped to the beginning of Jane's entries. Her first words were,

Mother is dead, but she did give me a last gift, her power over the rain. It was interesting how she did it, a small orb of light left her and

came to me and then her gift was gone. She did it under a moonlit sky and said these words: "I willingly pass to thee, my chosen daughter, that gift which my mother gave to me and her mother gave to her. By the power of the moon and the mind, let it be given." She asked me to copy them down since they worked. This leads me to think that she did not know if they would. We know now, for I have my mother's gift. It makes me wonder if we know enough about this gift for safety. I worry that all is not as it seems.

v   So, I could give my fillos all my gifts and have nothing left for myself. I wonder if that is what my mother did for me. I flipped to the back of the book and my mother's writing.

I did it. I reached her in time. The void I feel frightens me. I had not realized how much I relied upon my power from moment to moment. It kept me strong and confident. I feel the void in every conversation. I feel the insecurity. I am truly frightened. However, I am comforted, for I have done my work.

She had given her all to me. I had never understood this entry before now. She had given me her power of manipulation. I wondered if that was what made me so powerful. Perhaps I already had the gift, yet now I had it that much stronger. I also wondered if my grandmother had given me her gift. Perhaps that was part of their quest, to give up all their powers in order to make one exceptionally strong *fillos*, one who could rule. I was still at such a disadvantage despite all my power, because I did not have someone to guide me. I needed to know what my mother had planned for me.

September 1550

Ashridge House, Hertfordshire

Though I had been living in Hatfield, in September, Master Parry and I secured Hatfield in a more permanent manner. It seemed that Lord Dudley was happy to exchange the estate for a more pleasing one in Warwick.

Once the crown possessed it again, we exchanged for it a manor in Lincolnshire I had come by. The acquisition happened in the exact right moment, when I needed a bit of luck, for my spirits were down.

The fall began pleasant enough, and it was time to tour my properties, new and old, and make an accounting of furnishings and decor. The weeks seemed to fly by, as I traveled from one house to the next.

I also found that I threw myself into my studies and my prayer bench. It felt as if my relationship with God was on the mend, for I felt him now and then, in my heart, urging me onward in my pursuit of knowledge.

Robert wrote to me. This letter, however, was not what the others had been.

My dearest,

Now that I have the privacy of my own domicile—I am alone at court presently—I can say all that has been in my heart these last months.

I feel the sting of the days and weeks and months as they go by without my arms around you, my heart next to yours. I know what you did to me when last I saw you. I feel it pulling my will in a direction I cannot go. At first, I tried to hide my despair and I tried to love the woman I live with, as you so powerfully suggested. However, you need to know that your suggestion did not take hold. I saw you do it and I think that left me with a choice. The problem is, my dear, I will forever choose you. Do you not remember all I said to you? It will endlessly be true. Come what may. I love you. I love you. I love you forever. I have loved you for eight years with more parts of me than can be fathomed, there is nothing that could take your place in my heart, for there you are my wife. Forever. Always. Completely.

I must thank you, for I know what it must have cost you to suggest I love another. Righteous or not, never do that again! I will not be moved. We are for one another and none else. I mean that, and I live by it. IN ALL WAYS.
Expect letters a plenty from me while I abide in London, my darling.
Yours ever,
R

My heart almost leaped out of my chest with love and pure unfiltered joy. Robert. How faithful and glorious he was. And how fickle I was. I found that all the space I had placed between him and my heart over the last months closed, and all I could think of was him. I would do anything for him, including forsake all my morals and ideals and desire for the crown, for marriage, for children, and even I dare say for my standing with the Lord.

Robert melted me, down to the core, and all that was left at the center of my being was the relationship he and I had built together. I was who I was because of his love, his goodness, his faith and his friendship. I was his completely and I knew it once again.

I told myself I would never forsake that knowledge.

Of course, in the weeks to come of loneliness and solitude, with only my books and Kat to love me, I forgot the gusto of my declarations and went back to my prayer bench, knowing God was good and with me when I was with him.

December 1550
Hampton Court, London

I began to have dreams more and more. Most worthless tidbits: I had them about what I would learn in school the next day, or what cook would serve us for dinner. I saw visions of Edward on the throne watching a crowd of noble's dance. I also saw him ordering people about and sneaking sweets and kissing girls. That was disturbing. I saw Mary raging about and crying and being ill. I could neither confirm nor deny the truthfulness of these dreams, and I did not understand why I suddenly was having so many of them. And there was always the dream with the lightning and the water. I got that one at least once a month. Some were not worthless, some were helpful: I knew a scullery maid would be with child soon, I predicted a terrible windstorm, I saw Kat's horse throw a shoe and almost kill her when it broke its ankle. That horse got a new shoe the next day. I dreamt of Robert also, but I knew those were not from my gift. They were a study of his face and his body and I always woke up panting.

Being separated from my best friend, my love, my partner, and having to keep it to myself wrecked me. Still I knew this was the life I had made for myself; this was where my choices had led me. Fighting against it in my mind, dreaming of how the past could be different, was idiocy. I only could plan and hope for the future.

Letters from Robert indicated he, yet again, could not come to me, even though it was Christmas. He had mayoral duties to perform in Norfolk. And thus, our letters would be sparse again. A very small part of me was glad. I felt out of control when thinking about seeing him again. I did not know what I would do or how I would act. It frightened me. How would we be together? The same doubts clouded my mind. Had he been faithful to me even though he was living with a beautiful woman? He indicated as much, but could I believe him?

Still, we were constantly attempting to plan to see one another. Robert almost sounded desperate about it. I understood him.

We filled our letters with information. He did keep me informed of his duties and of the schemes he learned of. He told me that his father was soon to set him at Somerset, for he planned to have the duke executed. This disturbed me for my brother's sake. Edward has lost so much of his family already. I could not interfere with these schemes though, for Master Parry told me Lord Seymour had gotten himself into quite a bit of trouble, trying to rule over my brother and spending money like it was endless. All knew was that the game of princes and power was a dangerous one.

Robert said after the execution happened, his father would need him close by, for John Dudley himself would assume the Lord Protectorship. Robert's plans were to take a permanent residence in Somerset once it was empty, for it was not twenty miles from Hatfield and less than ten from my home at Enfield. It was even closer to the palaces in London where I hoped to be staying more often now. As happy as the closeness made me, it was shadowed by the news of the duke's execution. I understood the stakes, but I hoped Edward would run a different sort of regime.

I had been a hermit too long. I wanted my entire household of servants around me for this Christmas. I would enter London in style, and I informed everyone of my intentions. However, I was surprised when Edward sent a hundred of the king's horses to accompany my entrance. The letter he sent did seem to praise me highly for embracing the new religion my brother was heartily enforcing. The council even sent their regards with a note that they would like to receive me. I wondered if Mary was receiving the same attentions. Furthermore, I realized that I really had fooled everyone with my demure, saintly act, though it no longer felt like an act, but part of who I was now. I wondered if that is how it happened, character adjustment: you pretend to be what you esteem, until all of a sudden, you are not pretending anymore, but have become what you hoped for. I suppose it did.

I listened closely to the rumors and gossip, and there was not a hint of any of my old disgrace with Thomas, nor my new relationship with Robert. This made me nervous about seeing Robert all the more. I did not want to lose the person I'd become over the last few months to a love slave at the feet of the most wonderful man alive.

The day of my trip arrived. Roads were tolerable and so the journey to London was made quickly. It felt so good to be in the great city. All was frosty and chilled. The gardens were lovely stark sticks mixed with the beauty of the evergreens.

Mary came to me as I was settling in to my apartments, to invite me to attend mass with her. But, because I was still uncertain how the ebb of the religious tide in court went, I asked if I could perhaps join her later. "I still have so much to do if I am to see Edward and the council today."

"You are meeting with Edward today? I have been here a week and he has not seen me once," she said haughtily.

An idea began forming in my head, and so I decided to tread very lightly. "Well, I wrote to him expressing that I had not seen him. In fact, not since last Christmas have I beheld our brother the king. I feel he must have felt obligated to schedule a time for me because I was so upset over it." Hopefully that put all the blame on me and none on Edward, for he was only being obliging to a sister. "When have *you* last seen him, Mary?"

Her countenance did look better as she spoke. "It has not been longer than a month. But I was not in exile nor have I ever been, so it is understandable." She sniffed at me and gazed loathingly at my plain black dress. "I see that you are still playing the part of a virtuous maiden. How long will you keep that up?"

I knew that my face had shown my shock at her impudent statement, yet I was proud that my voice remained calm. "It is not an act sister. And I dress in this manner because it pleases me to be plain in the sight of my God." That, of course, was not the whole truth, but my pride would not let me divulge even the smallest measure of my act, or how it had truly changed me, to her.

She sneered at me condescendingly, "Well, you had better at least wear something freshly brushed or Edward will be put off by you."

"Yes, thank you, Mary," I said with haste. "Now, if you will excuse me, I will do just that." I did not even nod to her as I turned and left the room.

It was abuse after abuse with her, and I took it only because I had to.

Edward greeted me with affection and, though he had changed in mood, countenance and... size... it was a good change. He had grown so much and was starting to get wisps of hair on his chin.

"I believe it is time to get your man to give you a shave, Edward," I said with a laugh, and reached to give him a fond tickle on the chin.

"I am growing up, Bessy. But so are you. I bet you are as tall as a man. Let me see your feet, are you on stilts?"

I pulled my gown up and showed him my slippered feet. "Sorry, no, little brother. I am just cursed to be tall. We're both done being children, me thinks."

"Yes, I have been thinking on that, and have decided I should speak to you about marriage."

The blood drained from my face.

He continued, "I have some interested parties. Would you like to know who?"

I shook my head before I found the word. "Your majesty is so gracious, but Edward, may I please speak to you as a sister to a brother?"

His face looked shocked, but he nodded. "Of course. I want to make you happy, Bessy."

"Bless you, my sweet brother." I leaned toward him and lowered my voice. "Edward, what would make me the happiest in the world is for you to pretend that you don't have a sister named Bessy when suitors are about."

Edward took a step away from me. "I am confused, Elizabeth. Are you telling me you don't want to get married?"

The disapproval was evident. Thus, I moved forward carefully. "No, no it's not that, Edward. Of course I want to get married, someday. But, but I have everything I want right now. I am comfortable and enjoying myself. I just want a few more years of being free, and perhaps find someone worthy, but also someone I could love, for I do not have the same constraints on me that you do, as I am only third in line to the throne, and that is only until you have a child." I moved toward him and took his hand in mine. "Besides, there is no hurry. I am but seventeen." I pulled the light to me just in case my brother decided he would use his power to force me to do his will.

He wrinkled his brow as he thought hard. Finally, he pursed his thin lips and nodded, patting my hand affectionately. "Alright, Bessy, alright. I just thought... well, never mind what I thought. How about we strike an accord? You promise me we will have no more of the scandalous business that we had with my uncle Seymore, and I will wait upon you to give me the time, and perhaps the name of the young man you wish to be yours."

I smiled and hugged him. "Thank you, my king. I will try very hard to fall in love with someone politically advantageous." We both laughed at this and began walking down the foyer.

In the back of my mind, I wondered if I'd gone about the whole Robert thing in the wrong order. If I had just gone to my brother, would he have let me have Robert? My heart and soul drooped with the chance that another opportunity for Robert to be mine had perhaps been missed.

I saw Mary and Edward nearly every night. There were parties and frivolities constantly for the enjoyment of the court. I danced and sang and played my instruments to everyone's delight. I had a merry time. I met, or rather met again, an interesting man named William Cecil. We sat together and enjoyed a festive meal of boar and broth, mince pies, frumenty, plum porridge, and a Christmas pie of neat's tongue. I drank wine and cider and ate sugared pomegranate heart, all the while keeping a lively conversation up with William.

"Your brother the king is in much better hands now. I truly think Dudley will keep the finances right. He is quiet conservative by nature, has to be with all those children."

I did not let myself think of Robert as I nodded and smiled. "As long as he does not debase the coinage, I will be on his side. Father did leave things in a bit of mire, and the wars have not helped."

"My grandfather's beard, war is expensive. I would do all to keep it away. And you are correct, my lady, I myself will stay on his side in that case." He drank from his mug. "I do believe Edward will be a fine king. John is letting him have some leeway, and I believe the young majesty is taken with it. I feel some plans are afoot that will probably set Edward down a path gilded for a spot in history."

I smiled at myself, thinking of mine and Edward's conversation when I first arrived, how he had handled me. Yes, William was more correct than he could know. I glanced at him and saw a sly twinkle in his eye and realized, he did know. He nodded to me and smiled. I told myself that he was a fellow to keep a friendship with, for he was a man of information and of intelligence. A few moments of silence passed as we took one another's measure.

Then William said, "it is always good to have friends."

I smiled and nodded. "Yes, but best are the friends who understand how to be useful," I said carefully.

"That, but they must also know the importance of loyalty and mindfulness," he said, and took another sip.

I smiled. I liked this man very much. He was bold and sly.

He was a very interesting man, and had proved to be witty and loyal. In the process of the holiday, I enjoyed many such stimulating conversations with him. He talked to me of all that was happening in the political realm, and promised to be a friend with eyes and ears to keep me abreast of the new talks in court.

We agreed that Edward had needed guidance on how to deal with the religious issues father had left behind. William agreed with how John Dudley was helping with that.

My guess was that Edward, after so long of being under everyone's thumb (his uncle's), had decided to show his power in one area he felt passionately about. Though it was a risk—for the church of Rome was still very powerful and Mary promoted it at every turn—Father had done most of the heavy lifting. If Edward could just keep it going, he might be known as the most influential reformist of the movement.

This was his first act as king, and I saw him shouldering the burden of it. He was learning from the council and he was becoming wise. I was happy to think of what a great king he would become.

February 1551
Hatfield House, Hertfordshire

Back at Hatfield the winter felt exceptionally cold, yet I took many long rides through the crispy snow and slushy roads. I loved the time of freedom it brought me, and the air was so cold, it stopped my thoughts from making me unhappy. It wasn't long before I heard from Robert.

My love,

Father has bidden me to court. As his positions allow, he is free with his appointments in court. Though he has made no promises and wishes me to try my best to acquire after my own appointments, which I expected, I feel that he will have me in London often. I will be there from the middle of March until July.

I cannot wait to see you. It has been a year, and I feel completely lost without your face fresh in my mind to conjure up when I feel lonely. Father was right in many ways; the education I have received in business and the connections I have made this last year will benefit me the rest of my life, and yet, I cannot help but harbor malice for the man. Please relieve my suffering and say you will see me.

I love you. I love you. I love you forever.

Your Robin

I smiled and fingered the band of gold that encircled my fourth finger. I would go to London if I were on my death bed.

"Is that a letter from Robert?" Kat asked me from across the room.

I suppose now was as good a time as any to start the lie. I smiled, "yes, he is coming for a visit to London and wonders if he might see me. He would like to beat me soundly in a game of chess. I guess Amy doesn't have much of an aptitude for the game."

Kat smiled. "Well, we all know how that boy loves to beat you. What is the tally?"

I struggled to listen to her talk of Robert and I, and sniffed and looked away, not answering her.

Kat moved toward me, looking concerned. "Is this good? Him coming to visit? I know you have tried to be friends that correspond since he married, but you have not seen him for so long, do you think you are over your heart?"

Marriage had been good for Kat. She said this entire speech without halting or blushing once. "Yes, Kat. There is nothing else I can do. I gave it my best. It was not what the Lord wanted. But there is only one way to find out if I am healed or not." I folded the letter over and looked up at my companion. "Kat, I think I must see him. I must understand if I can be his friend as he wishes. If I can, then I can love another, someday. If I cannot, I will need to separate myself from him in all ways and let my heart heal." There was truth in this statement that I had not exactly known before the words were spoken. How would things be, and would it not be better if I merely cut things off with Robert? Truly just be his friend.

Kat came to me and held me then. "I am so proud of the woman you are becoming, Elizabeth, and the awareness you have of yourself." She pulled away and looked me in the face seriously for a few moments before saying, "I agree. Let's go to London and see what your heart tells you."

I awoke that night in a sweaty mass of linens. I saw in my dream what I would do to Robert when I saw him next, and God forgive me, I hoped it happened just as I imagined.

March 1551
Durham Palace, London

The whirlwind of packing and traveling and arriving and unpacking blew harshly through my life and left. In a week's time, I was settled in London as a nervous, frazzled, mess of a woman. The day I expected Robert, I fretted and paced all morning. By half past ten, I sat to collect my thoughts and fell so deep in that mire, I did not notice Robert's carriage arrive. My man opened the door and Robert stepped into my sitting room in all his beauty. His hair was longer in the back and he had a short, tightly trimmed mustache and beard, as was the style.

I melted inside. I bubbled and broiled. I wanted to scream at my butler to get out of the room. But he had seen I was alone and waited to be excused as he should.

"Robert, my friend," I greeted him, rising from my chair.

"Bessy, you dear girl," Robert answered with a short bow, "I mean, my dear princess."

I looked to my butler. "Thank you, Henry, that will be all."

He cleared his throat. "Shall I bring tea, my lady?"

I looked to Robert. "Tea?"

"No, I just had some. Thank you."

I looked back to my butler and he bowed himself out of the room.

The moment the door closed, Robert moved toward me and I toward him. But we stopped a foot apart. His eyes traced my face and I, his. I had forgotten how his face was exactly to my liking. How his cobalt blue eyes pulled at me and how his full lips were like a siren call. The heat and tension mounted with each heartbeat. My desire to touch him, kiss him, examine every inch of the body I worshiped in my dreams, tingled my skin. The anticipation of experiencing the most satisfying pleasure a human was allowed in this mortal life, with this man I loved so desperately, quickened my breath.

It was this horrid overwhelming overriding of my sense and reason and morals, this absolute feeling that I did not have any choice, that I was a creature of passion and desire that went off as a warning bell, a very quiet warning bell in my head.

I was certain Robert was experiencing the same difficulty as me, for one hand rose to touch me. I intercepted it and clutched at his forearm, simultaneously keeping him close, yet stopping him from pulling me to him. The strength to do so came from God. It had to, because I knew I did not possess it. He glanced at my hand and his eyebrows knotted.

Finally, the moment arrived where I had to choose. I had been given strength, but would I ignore it, or would I continue with it? It was my choice. Blood pounded in my veins, and slowly, ever so slowly, I used the minute amount of self-control I had within me to put my arms around his waist and lay my head on his chest, in almost a fatherly-type hug.

This action dammed the mounting tension.

And let the raging passion between us cool.

We held one another for an endless, and yet too brief minute. I found that I had begun to cry, and as per my usual, I snotted on his shirt. "I have missed you so very much, Robin."

"And I you, my Bessy." He bent and put his face deep in my hair, breathing me in. "Are you snotting on my new coat?"

I smiled but did not trust myself to look up at him whilst so close. "Perhaps."

He chuckled and squeezed me tight, while placing a kiss to my hair.

When I pulled away and stepped back, I saw that, though still in a state, he was in possession of his wits and control.

"Robert. We must speak about…"

"About our relationship. I know. I feel it keenly, my love."

A full shiver tickled up my back at his use of those words, but I had questions, doubts, concerns. "I am still your love, then?" I spoke the words so quietly, so gently, I feared he did not hear them.

He was quiet long enough for me to think my doubts reasonable.

When he did speak, his voice held fervor and anger. "Elizabeth. You are not asking me this question! I know you are not." He stared me down, his eyes flashing like polished blue agates. That gaze searched my soul like only God's angels could do. I could not hold it for long.

"What?" His voice rumbled with quiet desperation. "What is it?"

I began to cry again. I did not know how to tell him. I did not know what to say.

He moved to me and gripped my shoulders as he whispered, "Do you not love me? Or do you doubt my love? How is this possible?"

Now it was time for my eyes to flash. I pulled back from him and slammed my tears away with the back of my hand and glared. Love was not the question. Had he not felt the same thing I felt just moments before? No, the problem was making love. This thought made me blush.

I turned away from him and pressed my hands together, hard, dry washing them as they trembled.

"Robert," I whispered, keeping my back to him. "I cannot give you what you want. My heart has changed but not toward you. I love you, but I will not commit adultery with a married man. I thought I could do this. But I cannot. I…"

Robert pulled at my arm, turning me. He was smiling. I did not understand the expression, but then he was speaking.

"This is why. This is why. I knew God was leading me down this path for a reason, lending me strength." Taking my face in his hands, he let his thumbs caress my cheeks. "Elizabeth, you are my wife. My one and only wife. My one and only lover." He emphasized the words.

My eyes went wide. "What?" I asked.

His eyebrows knotted up again as he considered my expression. "Did you think I was spitting out prose... to what... seduce you? So, I could... have *you* before I got married to another? That I... lied to you?" His words were halting as he spoke his perception of my attitude. His hands dropped from my face. "Elizabeth?" He shook his head at me his mouth tight with anger. "I have gone an entire year, denying Amy any rights of a wife, for what... for this doubt in your eyes to be my homecoming? Elizabeth, you know me. I made a vow *to you*. The only vows I have ever made *were to you*. You are my wife! Yes, we live apart, we knew that would be the case. My commitment to the crown takes me from you as assigned mayor of Norfolk. Next year that commitment might be something different, but had I been assigned by the crown to be abroad for a year, all would be the same between you and I." He was angry now and pacing.

My mind raced with his words. My shock ran deep. "Robert, you lived with Amy for a year and never took her to your bed?" I asked shaking my head in disbelief. "Why?" I just could not understand it. "But I dreamed..."

He moved to me and took me by the shoulders and shook me. "I tell you now, Elizabeth, I did not. How could I? I love you, you foolish woman! I want you! The agony of waiting for you has been intense, but the Lord put it in my heart that I must, and he gave me the strength to persevere, and now I know why. It was to counter this doubt in your eyes with an unflappable no! I did not, could not be with Amy." His eyes traced my face and I saw the pain I had caused him. "So, tell me now, was it all in vain? Do you love me still? Are you mine?"

I sagged as his speech concluded. God had protected me also, he'd made me question, doubt, walk through my justifications. Just in case. But Robert had been faithful. Tears leaked down my cheeks, and I nodded and took his face in my hands, "Yes, Robert, yes. I never stopped, my faithful husband."

He assessed my face, capturing my eyes and when he was convinced, he crashed his lips into mine. I tangled my fingers in his hair and kissed him back with all the longing and passion I had held back before.

I had no idea how much time passed as we fell into one another once again. But when Robert was at his breaking point, he pulled me onto the couch. Once I settled beside him, I smiled and touched his check and kissed him more. His hands took my body, caressing me in a familiar, yet eager way. I pulled back. "We cannot do this now, my darling, not in the sitting room. Our reunion should be..." I left it hanging and Robert's eyes left mine as his head went back against the pillows. He took a few deep breaths to control himself.

Then he found my eyes again. "Yes, I understand completely, of course, what was I thinking?" He sighed and looked pained.

I nodded and pulled him to me for more kisses, but he did not respond.

Then he rolled from under me. Standing, he turned to face me. "I am sorry, my love. I need some time to recover."

I blinked at him, worried. "What is it?"

He blushed. "It is nothing. Just an ailment of the male disposition."

"What kind of ailment?" I raised my head, concerned.

He looked at me and said, "I will speak to you of this when we are in a different mood."

Closing his eyes and biting his lips together, he shook his head and looked away, his body wriggling uncomfortably.

"Can I help?"

His eyes flashed to mine. "Your words are giving me pain, my dear." I sat up and watched him walk carefully away from me. He placed a hand on the mantle and stood straight.

"You are worrying me, Robert." I went to his side and put my arms around him.

"Do not be alarmed, my dear. It is already getting better."

I went on tiptoe to kiss him just as Master Parry entered without a knock. Upon finding me in such a condition, he began to say, "I am sorry to intrude..." and then realized what he had seen. His face went white, then red. For he was very near a father to me.

I pulled the light to me as quick as a lightning bolt and hurled an orb of power. "You saw only good friends shaking hands when you came through that door." I whispered as the orb burst into his face.

I stepped away from Robert—who watched with fascination—and straightened my dress.

Master Parry turned to look at the door and then back at me confused, so I helped him out. "You were saying, sir?"

"I do not…remember." He turned in a circle confusedly. He cleared his throat and blinked. "Uhm," he looked down at his hand. "Oh, I have just received a letter for you. It is from Sir William Cecil, my lady princess, and I think that it must be of import." Master Parry always brought William's letters to me this way.

"What is so urgent that the secretary of state could not wait until you arrived this afternoon for your appointment with the king?" Robert asked, interested. "Unless he does not know you are coming, which would be rather odd."

I looked at Robert. "I think it odd that you know my schedule." He might know my schedule, but he did not know that William Cecil and I had started a friendship.

He smiled at me and winked. "I know many things, my lady." This made me laugh at him.

Master Parry shook his head at the both of us. "You two are as bad as children." He handed me the letter and turned to go.

But Robert in his ever-happy way, had to say, "why thank you, Master Parry, I hope I always can make a situation better with humor."

"You call that humor, boy? It's a good thing you don't have to earn your bread by it."

Robert laughed and so did I. "He's right you know."

Master Parry paused before he left. "Do I need to send Lady Katherine down?"

I looked from Robert to Master Parry with incongruity. "Why would you need to do that, it is only Robert, my oldest and dearest friend."

The old man huffed, "as you wish, my lady." And he closed the door behind him.

After Master Parry left, I turned to Robert, confused and alarmed by the almost fiasco, to see his eyes round and awed. I was still surrounded by the light of my power and I had forgotten how entrancing Robert found it.

Slowly, his hand reached up to touch my face. His fingers felt so warm, his gaze gentle and tender, and the attitude reminded me again how desperately I loved him.

When he looked at me like this, how could I not sag against his chest, how could I not pull his face to mine, how could I deny myself anything in moments such as these?

He kissed me so softly. Without passion, only with love. Sweet, honest love. It melted me.

Once my mind began working again, I found I had a letter in my hand, which prompted me to explain to him mine and William's friendship and correspondence, and how I felt he could be valuable in the future. Then, I opened the letter so we both could read it.

My lady Princess,

I learned that you were in London, would you do me the honor of visiting me before you attend on your brother, his majesty the king?

Yours,
W.C.

"I wonder what he wants." I asked.

"I suppose we will have to wait and see."

He smiled at me and we drifted for a while just looking at one another. But soon it was lunch and we both had other engagements. But, before he left, I took him on a little tour of the house. And we devised a plan for him to come to me after dark. After he kissed me goodbye, we walked out toward the stables.

"Shall we go riding tomorrow?" Robert, my husband, asked.

I beamed up at him, "I thought you would never ask."

~

Robert came, just after midnight as we had discussed. However, instead of a frantic affair of desperate kisses and ripping clothes, Robert spoke to me about the things that had been unexpectedly excruciating for him in my absence, and what had happened to him earlier in the sitting room. I pushed Robert to educate me on the male body, how it worked and what it needed. My respect for him grew immeasurably once he thoroughly explained it all.

We concluded that in our very strange arrangement, we might need to develop ways to help one another out with our desires. Ways that did not always involve a beautiful night under the sheets of my bed. Ways that might be messy and complicated and medical. It was a difficult task but, in the process of experimenting, I learned so much about him and he even explained to me my own body.

It was extremely enlightening.

After I understood what truly happened in conception, it gave me an idea on how to stop it. If human bodies were made of water, as I had been taught they were, and I could control water...

We did a bit of testing and found that, yes, indeed, I could stop the process needed for a child to be conceived. As a passionate student, this was all very interesting. As a lover it was a bit embarrassing. As a woman, a bit liberating. As someone who liked to excel, it was challenging.

After all was said and done, I rolled over to my husband exhausted, and put my head on his chest. "If I can love you still, and want you still, after this... shall I say, illuminating... yes, illuminating works... If I can still want you after this *illuminating* night, I think I will never be done with you."

Robert laughed and kissed me, then whispered, "precisely."

I smiled and thought about all that had happened to us. "Robert, how life would have been different had my father betrothed me to you when we were but youths."

He sighed, "oh, yes. I have wished for that so many times."

I smiled but could not tell him, if it weren't for me, we very well could have been betrothed back then. I did say, in a whisper, "now, I will burn in hell for all I have done."

"What have you done?" he asked, and sat up concerned.

I looked around at our tangled bodies and my expression must have said it all, for he responded, "this is not adultery, Elizabeth. If a husband and wife never consummate their marriage it is *ratum sed non consummatum,* which means, it is not a marriage."

"Ratified but not consummated." My eyebrows wrinkled up. "Robert, I have never heard of this?"

"Neither had I, for what kind of man would not consummate when he could?"

I looked at him and felt instant tears in my eyes. "Precisely."

He reached out and pulled a ringlet down and let it bounce. "I already had a wife. A wife I chose. A wife I loved. Why would I consent to marry another? I did not. I was forced. One cannot partake of holy sacraments under duress. So, I read the law and found what I had to do and then I did it. Amy understands. She was in love with a merchant's son when my father forced her to marry me. So, we understand one another."

I thought long and hard about this. It warmed my blood to the point of agony, but I could not think of how I wanted him forever, I had to ask. "Why did you not tell me this in a letter, you foolish man? It would have…"

"I know. I just did not want that to be what our visits were about. Conjugal visits. It seemed debasing. For you?" he scoffed. "But more, it was about loving you too much to get you with child. I know you have feared that your whole life."

That was it. I was speechless.

Of course he had to ruin the moment by adding, "However, now that we have the whole conception thing figured out, I will most heartily visit you conjugally as often as well may be." He laughed then and threw me onto my back, ravishing me with enthusiasm.

March 1551

Hampton Court, London

William! It is so wonderful to see you." I took the older man's hands in mine and gave them a good squeeze as he bowed his head.

"The pleasure is all mine, my lady princess. Was your journey pleasant?"

"It was. Thank you."

"Do you mind if we take a turn in the garden?"

"Not at all, that would be lovely." I took his arm and we moved that way.

As we walked, William began to speak. "My lady, I wonder if you might tell me your thoughts on the loss of the Antwerp market?"

"Shall I call you Master Ascham now?" I quipped at him.

He smiled. "Very good, my lady." But he did not go on and so I realized he meant it.

I cleared my throat. "Well, it is a rather big topic. Can you be more specific?"

"Yes, I suppose that would be helpful. Well, let's just say, what can we do about it now? What direction should we go in?"

"Well, I can tell you to look at the state of my broadcloth." I held up my dress. "It is not shoddy work, but it is not of the caliber I am accustomed. That is for certain. There is a lapse in the quality and volume. Imports from France, Italy, and Spain saturate our markets. Because we have not found a suitable replacement in the Hanseatic ports, our markets are suffering. We are getting a bad reputation and, as for myself, I only persist in buying English cloth out of duty."

After a half dozen steps, William stopped in his tracks, his eyes flashing brightly. "My lady. You give me exactly what I hoped for. An idea. Let me ask you, this duty you feel, do you think it would encourage you to buy patriotic colors in your cloths?"

I saw where he was taking this instantly. "I do believe a campaign could be launched, Lord Cecil, but I tell you now, the product needs improvement. Women will only go so far for their country."

"Or for their religion?"

I considered this. "Yes, that would add another layer of guilt." My tone was whimsical, and Cecil took it just as he ought.

He smiled at me and asked, "and what are your thoughts on debasing the coinage?"

I stopped. "No, sir. We have seen it before. It has small and quick benefit with harsh long-term consequences."

His eyes bright, he turned in a circle. "Uhm, thank you, my lady." He touched his vest pockets and again turned as if he were looking for something.

I caught his intention, he wanted to return the way we came. "Cecil, my dear friend, I am most tired, might we return?"

He looked at me knowingly and acquiesced. "Yes, of course. I am sorry for wearing you out."

⌒〜⌒

R obert and I took the horses out and about the grounds of Hampton after I had my meeting with the king.

"I had a pleasant visit with Edward," I told Robert. "He wanted my opinions of a few matters of state. I think your father has yet to prove himself to Edward and he knows I have good sense."

"That is good. Edward testing him is exactly as it should be, it will be what is best for the kingdom. My father is a lot of unflattering things, but one of his talents is with money. He knows how to do exactly what he should with money. I feel, at the very least, he will get us back on our feet."

"There are a lot of financial issues. William wanted to talk to me of that also. I hope that it signifies a long partnership between us all and the crown."

"Yes, I too, for that will keep us together."

I smiled at him and we rode in silence for a moment. "It does not bode well for Lord Edward Seymour, though. I fear once the people prosper under a more conservative leader, they will call for the Lord Protector's blood, and then my brother will have to kill his uncle and the man he is named for."

"I do not envy him." Robert shook his head. "We all rise and fall so easily in this game of princes, do we not?"

"We do, my love. We surely do."

Obviously, no longer contemplating the death of Edward Seymour, Robert laughed to himself. "But not you. There is no falling for you. How could you ever be made to do what you do not want? You can fill yourself with light and make your desires so."

I caught his meaning but did not want to discuss it at the moment. I had just spotted a rainbow in the distance. "Well, my love, I see something I want." I looked at him with a sultry glare. Then turned. "I want that," I pointed to the bow in the sky. "Let us test this theory of yours now, sir." I smiled at him mischievously and kicked my horse into a gallop.

All I heard was his call from behind me, "You cheat, madam."

I laughed as I raced over glen and hill.

Robert did not tell me, that first day we were together, that Amy had come with him to court. He did not tell me the second day, either. On the third day we were to have a dinner with Edward, the privy council, and a few other select guests, including Lady and Sir Robert Dudley.

When Master Parry said the name out loud, I could not hide my surprise. "Amy is here?"

Master Parry looked at his list and nodded. "Yes. Why is that so shocking?"

I turned away from him. "Robert did not mention it."

"I am sure he naturally assumed you would know."

I considered this. "Yes, I am certain that is why," I said distractedly.

It did not take me long to learn that Amy had come with Robert to London from the start, and was staying at Somerset with him. Robert never mentioned her. She did not go out into the public eye often, but I would have to spend an evening with her soon enough.

I dressed my best for the dinner that evening. Red crushed velvet and damasked silk, with my mothers' pearls at my neck. Edward led me into the dinner and sat me at his right, for we were the only royal people in attendance. John Dudley took the foot of the table, and his wife, Jane Dudley, was at his right. Guildford Dudley was on his mother's left with someone I did not know. I wondered at this, for Guildford was but a youth of sixteen; I should have seen it for an omen, but I did not.

And then there was Robert, sitting next to his father, with Amy on his left. I only looked at her briefly, but in that time, her pretty, heart-shaped face and blonde, naturally curly hair made me sick to my stomach.

Our table sat twelve, the remaining being William Cecil and his wife, Mildred, and William Paulet and his wife, Elizabeth. I sat next to William Cecil and I knew it for the trap it was. No one could know that William and I were in regular contact. I had to play this game John Dudley insisted upon and saw his gaze on me out of the corner of my eye. I greeted William, but instantly turned my attention to his wife who had Amy on her other side. I told myself it was not because I wanted to exclude Amy by taking her conversation partner.

The dinner went off rather well, except for Amy's continual way of touching my husband. How she laughed her pretty little laugh at him and how her eyes smiled at him. Robert was affectionate to her as well, looking into her eyes and finishing her sentences. They seemed to have all sorts of private jokes. It burned my soul to see it.

Amy was not without information and breeding, and it made me dislike her all the more, though I knew it was wicked to feel so. It was an overwhelming compulsion that started quickly and took me completely. By halfway through the dinner, I found I could barely say a word for fear of showing my anger and dislike to all around me.

My silence put my mind to thinking. Robert had not told me that Amy was in London. He had been attending me regularly. And now he sat at my brother's table, laughing with his wife. Though Robert and I talked, laughed, played chess, schemed, and rode horses together, the frequency was less of late and we were not together in the way he was with Amy. Perhaps we met conjugally too often. Perhaps the other parts of our relationship were falling by the wayside. As this thought settled, I felt an extremely painful blow to my heart. For in that moment, I knew what I was. A whore. I was a mistress. Having all the pains and joys of a lover, but none of the privileges of a wife. I was not a wife.

I truly was nothing.

Yes, when we spent time at my home, we were in our own world. I could control everyone around us. I controlled what we did, where we went, what we ate. I could even control the liquids in our bodies, rendering our private actions inconsequential. But here, in this scenario, I was without power unless Robert gave it to me. Instead, he gave all his power to his wife. And rightly so. I was a whore. Even my own mother would not lay with my father until he married her.

Livid, hurt and betrayed by my Robin, my best friend, my lover, I sat, stewing. Then, Amy wiped at Robert's face with her napkin in a very familiar way. I could take no more. I pulled the light to me with anger burning all the way to my fingertips.

The sudden appearance of my light drew Robert's eye to me. He had not even looked at me the entire evening.

I saw fear in his eyes as I looked from him to Amy. My face must have been a glowing storm head, for he shook his head at me imploringly and, thinking fast, addressed me.

"My Lady Elizabeth. I hear you got a new colt. Please, I am longing to hear all about it. We have not gone on one ride this whole week. Might I be so bold as to invite myself over to come see the little beast?"

I couldn't respond.

He swallowed, giving me a hard look, and continued. "And then might I be so bold as to request the honor of riding the countryside with you and Mrs. Ashley?" Here was Robert the courtier I knew so well, and *disliked* so much.

William whispered to me before I could answer, "carefully, my lady. Bridle your passions, for all can see you."

I looked at William astounded. Did my dear friend and confidant know more than he should? Shocked into calm, I watched as William moved his eyes and head slightly back toward Robert, indicating I needed to address his question before social niceties were made awkward with my silence.

I cleared my throat and looked at Robert, in possession of myself. "Yes, Sir Robert. You know that my stables are forever open to you, for you are the dearest of friends and I trust you completely to care for any animal you meet." There was fire in my eyes and Robert did not miss my double meaning, but I could tell he was confused by it.

How could he not understand that his actions with Amy were hurting me? It frustrated me to no end. My mind repeated over and over again the word *whore*. I could not shake how very unhappily unattached I was. I could not stop my mind whirling and imagining the most dreadful things. I felt almost possessed and truthfully, it scared me. So much so, that by the time I returned to my rooms, I had all but decided to give Robert up. It was fatalistic, I knew, but I just could not think of how to move on from here.

"Do not touch me, Robert." I said to him as he slipped into my rooms that night. I was waiting for him, still dressed. Still frustrated, and yet resolved.

"You know that it had to be that way. This is the part I play. If I thought you did not understand, I would have put you on your guard."

"I cannot do this right now. I am too angry."

"Elizabeth, I am at a loss. What did you think I would do with Amy? Ignore her? Hate her in front of all my relations and hers? I have to play the part. I do it for us, so that no one suspects. So that we can go on the way we have."

I looked him in the eye and my voice became very quiet. "That makes me nothing more than your whore."

Robert's face drained of blood. His eyebrows wrinkled with confusion and concern. He swallowed and looked away. He could not hold my gaze. He could not stand against the truth in the words. He looked down. He did so out of shame because he knew I was right.

"Our love can be everything to us," I continued in the same quiet, measured tone that held no love, nor understanding. "but it means nothing out there." I flung my hand vaguely indicating the out of doors. "If we look at it carefully, I am more a mistress than a wife." I turned away from him and whispered even quieter. "And I cannot be thus any longer. I will not." I step even further away from him, "It has long pricked my conscious and my pride. I do not doubt you. I know we are committed to one another, but..."

Robert moved toward me, "Elizabeth, please..."

"You will hold your ground, sir." Rebuking him coldly, I pulled the light to me.

Anger and hurt flashed in his eyes, but he stayed in his spot.

His face milled and vacillated. "It does so to me as well, prick my conscious. But that is because the traditions of our fathers have willed it so. Yet, I know we are right. I love you. You are my wife."

"I am not your wife, Robert. She is. So, stop saying it. I cannot go on as we have. I know it shall be difficult. I know I will hate myself in the morning, but I have to at least try. I cannot be made to feel as I was tonight ever again. I think I would rather be dead. Unless..." Then my passion overcame me, and I stalked to Robert, I grabbed him by his vest and told him. "You are mine, Robert. Mine! And you act like you are mine. I have given everything inside me to you, in spite of my fear, in spite of my morals, in spite of my god, in spite of our laws. I sacrifice it all to be with you." I knew I sounded like a lunatic, but I could not help it.

He pulled me to him and gathered me to his chest as I clutched at his back, angry and desperate. "I cannot do it, Robert. I cannot." He held me until my breathing calmed down.

When I pulled away from him, I saw what was happening on his face. He looked like he always had when we were in school together and he could not figure out a translation, lost and uncertain. He looked like he had been punched in the gut, yet all he could do was stand there, silent, staring at me.

After a few moments of his mind working, his eyes narrowed the slightest bit, and that was my only warning of what was to come.

"I am very sorry to have distressed you this evening. I am sorry for all you have sacrificed and given up. I am sorry that you forgot that I must play the part of husband in front of all. I am sorry that you misunderstood that I am protecting you by doing this, for if my father found out our relationship, he would not stop to think before he tucked us both away in a nice, cold, cell. Not to mention you would be ruined." He paused and his mouth went tight. "But I am mostly sorry that you doubt me, after all I have done to control myself and that you cannot control yourself." He straightened his vest then and bowed before leaving the room.

I was left speechless.

I did not see Robert for six months after that, though we did communicate via letter. Nothing about our fight. Nothing about our relationship. Only state business, such as Durham house needing to be given up so that the privy could meet there, and the French ambassador taking over that house for the unknowable future.

I had done it to myself. I saw that right away, but I was too proud, too confused, too uncertain of what I really wanted, to tell him my thoughts. So, I got used to having him as a pen pal only.

August 1551
Hatfield House, Hertfordshire

I received word that the sweating sickness had struck. This sickness was different than the plague—which infected the peasants en masse—it was no respecter of station. It killed rich and poor with equal malice and within one day. Which meant it would not take long for the nobility to exit London and sequester themselves in their country houses.

I, along with all my house, retired to Hatfield where we hid and prayed that we would not be stricken.

Though I still felt resolved against Robert, and though I had not seen him (which probably was for the best) I worried over him. He was back and forth to Norfolk; I hoped it would not tire him out, for he needed to be strong with such a terrible sickness afoot.

The generous part of me hoped that he was happy in his new life and that he had given himself up to his wife.

Of course, that was a very small part of me.

I also had a small part of me that hoped Amy would contract the sweating sickness and this nightmare would all be over.

But that was a very small part of me, too.

October 1551

Hatfield House, Hertfordshire

William sent me a letter warning me in his special way of the happenings in court. I used the information I received from all my sources to piece together the truth, though. Everyone was saying that Lord John Dudley would have his way. And soon enough, Edward Seymore, the old Lord and protector, and uncle to Edward, my brother, was condemned to die, and John Dudley would be made the official Lord Protector and Duke of Northumberland.

Robert did not write me until after his father became the Lord Protector.

PART II:
THE FALL

March 1552
Durham Palace, London

Edward Seymour had been dead for two months. Lord John Dudley had taken the job to the finish, and now completely stood in my brother's uncle's place as protector of the king and kingdom, and first among equals in the privy council. So far, Lord Dudley seemed amenable and actually facilitated opportunities for Edward to make his way as king. Supporting him in his religious reforms and financial conservatism, instead of carving out success for himself as Seymour had, John, in all ways, tethered his success to that of my brother and the hope of his long reign.

Lord Dudley did act as the dictator of the privy schedule, and that lent him much control, which he used without hesitation. He placed people that supported his agenda in the council and employed all his children to involve themselves in matters of state, but he also respected the king and did all that Edward wanted.

With the regime change came perks; Robert was now living in London at his new residence, Somerset palace, Edward Seymour's old house. It had been a year since Robert's and my fight. It was never talked of, but we had fallen into a sort of friendship and partnership that, though not as all-consuming as our affair had been, was in fact more cordial, fulfilling, and safer. Which was good, for it was a busy time,

Edward now being a young man and making his own way. The kingdom was a-flurry with changes. I was required at court to council him more. But so was Robert.

I made my London home of Durham Palace my main residence. It was a wonderful house and so very conveniently placed near court.

Robert was due for a visit today. This would be the first time he had come to my home in a year, the first time we would be alone in a year, and so I waited nervously at the fireplace in the sitting room facing the street.

Master Perry knocked and brought me in a letter. "It is from William." He explained shortly and handed the paper over.

"Thank you, Thomas, for always seeing that I get these letters promptly."

"Of course, my lady. You know that I am your man in all such matters."

I smiled at him and nodded as I broke the seal and unfolded the paper.

My princess,

I hope you are in good health. I am sure you are wondering why this latest letter to you is coming in so strange a form, since I will enjoy the great pleasure of seeing you this evening at St. James. I needed to tell you that your brother is unwell again. After the sweating sickness, he just has not been the same. This information is not public, obviously, so please do not speak of it other than to myself. Moreover, you must not be alarmed I assure you it is but a fever and a cough. The lord will bless us with the king to rule us for many years to come, I am certain. However, I fear that it has made Lord Dudley uneasy, and I see and hear things that make me wonder if he is not making a contingency plan should the most unfortunate of all circumstances occur.

All I can find out is that he desires the throne to go to neither Mary nor yourself. I can describe what that means, but I know you to be far more insightful than myself, and therefore I will leave out the details of my thoughts. Furthermore, if such a treasonous plan is put forth, I can-

not help but wonder at who would fill the vacant throne.

I would ask you to take care.

Also, I am sending this to Durham Palace, but I wonder if you will not be long there, for I have heard a report that this same Dudley plans to move you out and take the place himself. Be wary. If he can best you in property, he will take it as a sign he can best you in all things.

I hope to meet with you privately to discuss this information more thoroughly, at your convenience of course.

Best wishes,
William C.

This was alarming news, the kind I was barely able to get my mind around, as Robert, my beautiful Robert, was let into my room. In my state of shock and fear, I merely handed the letter to Robert without a word and moved to the couch.

This news caused me concern, for John had proved himself capable of killing those that opposed him. When he finished reading, Robert took a seat, the blood drained from his face.

His reaction worried me. "Robert, am I in danger?" I asked, as he sent the paper into the fire flames.

He was silent for a few moments before answering. "No, no. My father does not keep me up to date on all his plots, but I have heard nothing of this. Not a word." He stood and began pacing, as was his way. "But, just to be cautious, we should discuss it. If anyone would be in danger, it would be Mary, for she is already clandestinely gathering her Catholic followers to her. She is ready at a moment's notice to fight for the crown. Shameful as it is when the king is not yet dead. Still, you have not made bid for it. Mary speaks openly about what she would do if she were to be queen. You do not."

"But the problem is, Robert, how will they get the power to choose a different queen than what is set up in the law? My father's third succession act legitimized mine and Mary's claim to the throne. I stand before you third in that line, all the world knows it, and calls me princess." I began to pace now. "And further, who would they have to take our place? Jane? Margaret? How could they be better than I, who was raised at the foot of a great king?"

Robert thought. "I do not know. But I do know one thing about the council. If there will be a coup, it will be a religious one. It will not be about you personally. They fear a revitalization of Catholicism under Mary, naturally. It would destroy all their work."

I stopped pacing, and closing my eyes, I pulled the light to myself. After my mind cleared, I brought forward the facts I knew. They needed a new sovereign they could count on. Robert said any coup after Edward would not be personal but religious. I sympathized with Protestants, though I did not show it openly. Lord John Dudley saw, for he knew I did not go to mass. Their problem was Mary.

How to get rid of her? As women, Mary and I were sort of peas in the same pod. They could kill her, or both of us. I do not think they could kill us so easily or with Edward's blessing. So that was out, for now. The only possible way I could see to get Mary out of the way was to again declare her a bastard and have Edward go along with it. If that were the case I would not be saved from the same insult, for how could they say one daughter was and the other wasn't? With Edward's lack of producing an heir, the throne would go to our cousin, Jane Grey, whose pedigree was sure, and she was a very Protestant girl. Jane's future husband would be king consort. And since Jane was presently unwed, the powers that be could carefully choose her husband and thus, with her docile nature, would be choosing the next king as well.

I gave Robert the seed of the idea I just received. "They will have to find a way to dispose of both Mary and I if they are going to do it. Remake us into bastards. The law does not allow for them to ignore an heir for their religious persuasion. They will put Jane on the throne and choose the king for her."

Robert stared at me as he always did when I was filled with light. It was a look of ecstasy, like there could never be anything as glorious as I was. It only lasted until my words were finished, but still the thrill it sent up my spine… he had not looked at me in such a way for a year. He shook his head and focused. "I see how you must be right, what a horrid plan. But I do not understand how they can make sense of it, for if they want to talk of legitimacy, Mary is the only *legitimate* heir. They cannot have it both ways."

"Yes, if we all want to be technical and ignore all the rules and traditions my father ripped to shreds, Edward is just as much of a bastard as I am. And yet, because he is a male, they do not question his place."

Robert added, "to do this, they will have to get Edward on board, and he will never do it. He has to see the truth of lineage as we do. He would be cutting off his own legs if he nullifies the succession act."

"Yes, he will have to twist the law until it is broken, not to mention betray his sisters in a most awful way," I confirmed.

"Do you think he could do it?" Robert asked quietly.

I thought. "I do not know. It has been done before. And religion is very important to him. Plus, for this to even be an issue, Edward will have to be dead. And what do the dead care for?" Then with my voice saddened by the idea of this treachery, and by worry for the decisions my brother might need to make, I asked, "how sick is Edward?"

"I do not think it is this exact sickness that has the council worried, they are all very tight-lipped about it. But I think it more the fact that he keeps getting sick."

"He did thus even as a child," I noted.

"Yes, I remember. But he always pulled out. He is a robust person, like his father."

I smiled. "Yes. Let us just pray for him. Let us pray and hope that he will live long and well."

Robert narrowed his eyes at me, not in an angry way, but in a confused way. He had something on his mind but did not want to tell me.

"Robert?"

He shuffled around, looking down at the floor, chewing the inside of his cheek like he did when thinking very hard on something.

"What is it?"

He took a breath to speak but then stopped and looked away. I moved closer to him as if the last year had not happened, and it was as if it hadn't. My arms ached for him. My body warmed thinking about touching him. Still, I only laid my hand on his forearm.

His eyes glittered as he looked at me in so profound a way, I felt my heart race into a gallop.

Then I realized I still had the light around me, so I let it go.

He smiled, but did not look away. "You are rather distracting in that condition."

I stepped closer, capturing his eyes, not allowing him to look away. We stood there, gazing at one another. So much between us. So much unsaid. Love and lust denied. Heat and passion ignored. Neither of us moved. We only breathed.

Finally, I whispered, "tell me, sir, what is troubling you?"

He pulled his arm away from my hand and, after glancing away for a breath or two, looked down at me. Taking another deep breath, he said, "this is a horrid thought, that is why I hesitate, but I recall a time when you told me you felt very certain *you* were meant for the crown. That it was your calling. So, perhaps this sickness is how God's plan will be revealed to us."

I pulled further away from him, blinking at the truth I had forgotten. Both my siblings would have to perish for me to be queen.

Once Father died, Edward was king. He was so young, he seemed to be destined to rule forever. The idea of me wearing the crown had slipped away quietly to the place were all childish dreams go to die.

Furthermore, I had been so happy with my life. With Robert. My properties. My family close by. The handful of people that loved me. I was involved enough in politics through Lord Cecil to keep me sharp and useful. I had forgotten my old hunger. My old ambition.

I walked back to the fire, my mind whirling over Robert's words. Yes. I had felt that I would be queen. I knew that was God's plan for me. I felt it now as strongly as I had then. But how? Where these events bringing that reality to pass? How were they hindering it? And what could I do about it?

Once again, Robert set me on a path I would not have trod without him. I knew that being queen was in my future. I did not know how it would come to pass, but I knew that if it was to be, I needed to be ready. Perhaps it was time to remind everyone who I was and what I could do. But how?

The opportunity presented itself soon enough.

At this time, Master Parry informed me that someone was inquiring particulars about my property at Durham place, as William Cecil had hinted. Durham was a property very convenient and large, stately and well-dressed—now that I had reconstructed it—with opulence to covet. Truly it was my finest property and one meant for royalty. It had sentimental value to me, for it was lived in by the Boleyn family, and Edward had granted it to me as it was a requisition in our father's will. That made this inquiry into my property a political move, one of the sort I did not want when there were those questioning my legitimacy.

It was John Dudley. I knew it. He was playing the game and attempting to take me down a notch.

William's warning now made sense; I would have to thank him. For I was summoned to court, and if this had been sprung on me there, who knows what mess I would have gotten in. Time for analysis would prove vital.

If John had good reason for wanting the use of the house, as in for a matter of state perhaps, I could not deny him. He might have that, I did not know. I needed more information.

I swiftly wrote to William. The note had two words, *"Durham terms?"* I sent my boy off with a coin and pressed him to get an immediate response.

Not two hours later my boy returned. I hastily opened the small note and read:

"Perhaps trade for Somerset? He can force the matter. French ambassadors."

He did not address this or sign it. Somerset was Robert's home at present and not exactly in town. It did not appeal to me at all. But he could force the matter, which meant he did not *have to* trade me at all.

How could I use this? I needed to play the game. Give and take. I had played chess all my life. I knew that one must give for the greater plan, but one must do so from a position of strength. This property issue could be just such a situation, if I handled it correctly.

But how? How could I assert myself to Lord Dudley in a small thing, so that he would not think me incapable of fighting for my rightful place? But I also had to give him what he wanted. I gathered the light to me and waited for my mind to work out a plan.

⁓

I s all in readiness?" I asked Master Parry.
"Yes, my lady."
I looked around the courtyard. Before me was every last servant and armed man in my employ. They would march beside me to St. James. This large procession would make the statement I wished. I was the old king's daughter, a princess, and I would not be discarded so easily. After arriving with force, I would benevolently bargain away part of my birthright, asking only a small thing in exchange. Give and take.

Something I did not expect happened, as if God were making a statement himself. Crowds of people saw my banners and flocked around me, crying out my name with love and joy. They followed my procession all the way to the steps of St. James where Lord John Dudley himself stood waiting for us.

I found that very brave of him, for what if I were there to kill him and take over the throne? Then I saw Robert lurking and knew—as he winked at me—this was his doing. I smiled triumphant.

I stepped out of my carriage and gave him a warm 'no, I am not trying to start a revolution' smile. "Lord Dudley, how are you?"

"I am well, my lady princess. Only awaiting you, and I see you come in style." He appraised my guard.

"Yes, well, I thought I had better bring them. They needed airing out. And one can never be too careful, these are perilous times." I looked around pensively. "I feel something in the air, Lord Dudley. I am uncertain as of yet what it is, but it begins to taste like treason." I splayed my hand out toward the people and waved, to which they cheered loudly. "As princess, and as a person invested in self-preservation, I must play my part in protecting the king and the royal line." I put emphasis in the exact right spots so that it was impossible for him to mistake my true meaning... unless he was dim-witted.

He eyed me askance and said, "you are very wise, my lady."

"I just knew you would understand my intentions, my lord." I took his outstretched arm and let him lead me into the palace.

He smiled. "Rational people must never wonder when others understand them, and we all know you to be exceptionally rational, my lady."

"You flatter me, my lord. I have done nothing to deserve such praise." I knew that this would come to a head soon and I hoped to open the way for him, so I began to think hard on what I could say.

"You do deserve it. You are a very clever young woman. I have always found you thus, if you will remember."

"Yes, I do remember. For did you not once compare me to a clever *son* of yours?" I purposely baited him now.

"I did, my lady. I also recall apologizing for the insult, though I do not think you would take it as thus now. You have formed a very great... friendship with him, have you not?

His pause on the word friendship bothered me, but I did not let it trip me up, though I wondered what he knew. "Indeed, my lord, I would not take *much* offence. I find Robert to be most excellent company, and he *is* a dear friend of mine, though he is *still* a man." I laughed obligingly. "In truth, I suppose I owe you for that foresight. Tell me, my Lord, is there nothing I can do to thank you?"

The man looked shocked by the offer. Did he know that I knew what he wanted from me? He was not an idiot. He would take advantage. "Well, yes, my lady... if you are serious? There is something that you could do for me. I have a business proposition for you; you could look on it favorably for me." He cleared his throat after I motioned for him to proceed. "You must know that I recently acquired Somerset House."

"Yes, well, you are the de facto Lord Protector. You should have such a property; it is fitting your new station." I hoped very much to drive home the point that he was not the king. That I outranked him.

He grunted and eyed me suspiciously. "Do not take me wrong, I am very grateful. As you know, it has been useful. It is just, with my duties here, it is not a convenient place for me to set my family. I'm sure you understand."

"Oh dear, trouble already? I thought this new position would be a boon to you in all aspects." I smiled sweetly. I could tell I was disarming him with my comments. "I suppose sometimes things do not turn out as planned."

He went on slowly, "yes, I see your point. But back to the business at hand. I would like to propose that we exchange Somerset for Durham. I am willing to compensate…"

Whatever he wanted to give me I wanted him to double it, so I broke in before he could even finish his offer. "Lord Dudley, you cannot be serious. Durham is my favorite London home. One my father left to me as princess of this realm. My station demands such a residence, and I have no wish to have another estate outside the city. I already have Enfield and Hatfield, as you know."

He paused in his walking to look at me. After assessing my face, he chose to sweeten the deal, not assert his power. This was why the grand show was necessary. He was not dealing with a royal female prat; he was dealing with Henry Tudor's daughter.

I went on, giving a little so he would not feel run over. "I do understand that it might be a better location for you, but I did not think Edward Seymour found it a distasteful distance. And I have heard you are an excellent horseman. Besides, I do not wish to be parted from Durham only to cast Robert out of Somerset, for is it not his residence now? No, my Lord, I could not do that to him, and I dare say I do not think you would have brought up the idea had you remembered your son."

Dudley's eyes narrowed for a fraction of a second, and I knew he knew that I had just gotten the upper hand. However, his smile returned with vigor, "My lady, I beg you not to worry over Robert, for I have already thought of a scheme to keep him here. He will not be separated from… from London, never you fear. And I have a wonderfully generous offer for you, will you not at least listen to it?"

I smiled inside. I wanted Robert to stay, and so he would. Triumph number one. "Well then, if I have your word as a gentleman that Robert will be allowed to stay in London, and in a comfortable situation, mind you, I suppose I would not feel so guilty about listening to your offer." I let my smile show then and Lord Dudley was affected by it, I could tell.

"I know, my lady, that you have just recently finished some refurbishment to Durham, and thus, I propose that I help you financially with the changes that will be needed for Somerset. Say a payment of nine hundred crowns? Do you feel that sufficient?"

It *was* a generous offer, and in all other circumstances, I would have felt glad of it, but I had to play my hand here. So, I screwed up my face a bit in thought. "Yes, you are right, Durham would afford you a much better situation; and though it pains me to let it go, I suppose it will do you much good. Perhaps if I can do you much good now, you will feel friendly toward me should I ever be in need."

"You are very shrewd, my lady." He said seriously.

"Why, thank you."

"So, we have an agreement?"

We entered the sitting room. "We have an agreement. I will have Master Parry speak with your man tomorrow." Letting go of his arm, I sat down in the plush chair next to the fireplace and took a moment to be happy. I had gotten the two things I wanted. Robert to be comfortable, and for me to come out the other end not looking like John had forced me into this arrangement… and the large sum of moneys was a boon not to be ignored. The moment passed and soon I looked to John with concern.

"Now, my lord, tell me truthfully… how does my brother?"

A shocked look again graced the man's face. "He is well as can be, my lady."

I raised an eyebrow slightly and said, "I am glad to hear that his cough and fever have subsided. That is what you are telling me by saying he is well… is it not?"

Dudley's face blanched. He knew I knew, and thus did not want to lie to me. "You are right, my lady, there is no harm in you knowing the particulars, only please do not talk with others about it. No one is to know, by order of the king. He has the measles and perhaps also small-pox."

I felt the blood drain from my face. This was much worse than I thought. "God save us!"

He went on. "The council is in a frantic state for it is looking to be a bad case. We are all praying that he will pull through, but if he does not, there is much to be planned since he has no heir…"

"This is grave indeed. I can see why you are keeping it quiet. I will join my prayers with yours, my Lord. My poor brother. How very inconvenient it must be to be the king and to never be able to get ill without everyone talking of what your demise might mean." Touched, I rose and stood before him. "Fortunately, in this case, the path ahead is well laid out. My father saw to that. The succession act states Mary will be next, and thus there is no need for the council to make any contingency plans. Though we hope for the best, it is in the hands of God and our rule of law, Lord Dudley."

He wiped at his brow, assessed me some more and then continued, "I am hopeful that the doctors are wrong and that it will be but a few days of suffering for his majesty."

"Just between you and I, I pray that the good Lord makes it so, for candidly, I would not look on Mary as queen with any degree of pleasure. Still it is in God's hands, and I would follow the law as a good subject."

Lord Dudley's eyes widened at this admission. He spluttered and I decided I needed to move the conversation along.

"Am I to see him? My brother, the king, I mean. He summoned me," I clarified, as John continued in his shock. Good. I hoped I'd given him a sound tongue lashing.

Finally, he stated, "not today my princess, I fear. That is why you are at St. James. His majesty the king is in Whitehall and we have closed that off."

Now it was my turn to be confused. "So, why was I summoned my lord?"

"To talk with me, of course." This statement had a very negative impact on me.

Lord Dudley summoned me? Lord Dudley! Who did he think he was? He does not get to summon me, a princess. This changed the meaning of my procession and the proceeding negotiation in enumerable ways. No wonder I had gotten the upper hand. He thought I knew that it was he who summoned me, and I had come without complaint and was thus asserting my dominance with the procession. I just showed him I had no clue what game was at foot here. The foolish princess really was just "airing out" her men. It was a small thing, but I could see that all the clout I had gained in this encounter was ruined. Curse Cecil and Master Parry, they should have told me.

I noticed a smug look in his eye as he said, "however, since our business is finished, you are welcome, by the king, to stay at St. James for the duration of the month, unless the king's condition gets better. In which case, he has a great desire to see you at Whitehall." He fluffed the lace at his wrist and said, "Well, my lady, if you will pardon me, I have other business to attend to." He was dismissing himself from my presence.

I could do nothing but nod my head, and he bowed out of the room. He had won.

The annoyance at the presumptuous man and my blunder drove me into the interior of St. James, where I stomped along the corridors filled with portraits of my father's family, fuming and muttering under my breath. As I looked down the long line of beautiful men and women who made up my ancestry, I burned on the inside. The mountains of injustice and knavery, and the anger at my noviceness, were about to crush me.

First, that man had summoned me. Not invited, summoned, as if he was the king. He planned to take my crown, that was obvious from our conversation. What else was he planning? I needed to know. I paced back and forth. But that was not all he had done. John Dudley had married Robert off, and I would never forgive him for it. He planned on marrying me off when I was but a girl. He probably still planned to marry me off. Then, he had taken Hatfield and now he takes Durham and gives me Somerset, knowing full well that I could not truly refuse him, and purposely ignoring how these actions would force his son to relocate. It was as if he knew how Robert was needed in my life, and he held him over me like a noose.

To complicate my mood further, Edward was sick, truly sick, and very well might die. I felt the tears coming as I looked up to the portrait of my father and suddenly, I felt everything crashing down on me.

I rushed to the chapel that was the majority of St. James and found a bench. Bowing my head, I cried mightily unto the Lord to save me from the feelings of hate and anguish that filled my soul.

Greed had made me take Durham Palace, and now it was taken from me and I mourned it. I foolishly wasted my chances to make Robert mine when I had the love of my father and his power to back my claim, and John was punishing me for it now, I was sure of it. That same foolish, younger self that feared marriage and children, coveted the crown and pleaded for God to tell me how it was to be mine, and now... Edward was sick. Again, my discovery of this afternoon resonated with me...the crown would only be mine when my brother and my sister—the only two people in the whole world I was so connected to—were dead.

I did not want that to happen. Death was horrid. By the time I was barely a woman, I had lost Father and Mother. Then my second set of guardians, Katherine Parr and Thomas Seymour, were dead next. Yes, some members of that group were wretched, but nonetheless...I had only Mary and Edward left. They were my family in its entirety. And one might die soon.

Of course, I had Robert and Kat, and perhaps Master Parry. They were large in my heart. But it still felt pathetic that in all the world, those were the only people who loved me. Why was the list so short? Was I so hard to love?

Imagining Edward and Mary's death cut me to the bone and

broke my heart. The tears ran down my face. I pulled the light to me, so that I might be comforted. I put my face in my hands as tears ran profusely, draining all my hurt, sorrow, and repentance into that fragrant bench of oak.

After a very long cry and much contemplation, the Spirit of God descended upon me. I felt it, as if a shawl of love came and wrapped around my soul. It chastened me for my weakness, then it healed me. Once again—for I felt as if I was always deciding this and then going back on my word—I determined to be a woman ready to let God guide her, instead of fighting God's will. When it was time for me to start my own mission, He would let me know, and I would be ready and willing.

December 1552
Whitehall, London

The year passed quiet and quick. I moved about between my houses. Attempted to play a part in court. Kept contact with William Cecil and Robert. They were my eyes and ears. Edward would go in and out of sicknesses. When he was having a bout of feeling his old self, he would want to convince all that he was well and thus would have dinners, dramatization, and voids mixed with political activism.

He drove the council to madness with his need to create a more secure border between England and Scotland by commissioning Scot's dike.

He spent more money than he ought, while laying plans for establishing grammar schools all over the country.

I believed Edward was picking the things he most cared about and wanted to see them done. It was almost like he thought he was going to die, and was thus compelled to work hard. It frightened me.

Robert and I never saw one another unless it was in a gathering and then, we only spoke casually. I could not be around him. Though the pain of our estrangement and our uncharacteristic void in face to face communication affected me deeply, I rediscovered Robert as a written confidant and friend. We wrote daily to one another. And I knew from William's letters that he and Robert were in one another's confidence.

For the winter, whilst Edward was well, I stayed with him at Whitehall, but so did many of the privy council and family members, including Robert.

Robert and I in the same house? I did not know what that would be like.

I did not need to worry, for Robert brought Amy to court with him again. It made sense. Somerset house was now mine, the paperwork having gone through, and Lord Dudley's scheme made clear to us all. I was shoved off and Robert was to be kept at court, where he would be close at hand. Lord Dudley kept his son busy and with so many people capable of spying (this clandestine activity half the draw for many to stay at court), it was a precarious time indeed. I was glad Robert and I did not have a relationship to protect.

Not a few days into the holiday, though, John Dudley had a strange demand for me, and I felt something treacherous in it. He wanted to send Amy to Somerset, to stay. Robert's wife to stay at my house! John had already forced me to stay out of my own house for a year, the house he traded me, but never really gave up, the house so far removed from court it was not suitable, the house in need of redoing, for he knew I had no intention of removing Robert from the premises. But Robert was not there any longer. Did he just expect my generosity to have no bounds?

This essentially would make him the master of Somerset and Durham, and me the master of none. Furthermore, he did not give me a choice. So, after the Christmas holiday, Amy would be gone living at my house. And I would be here at court, subject to the whim of Lord Dudley and Edward.

My guts twisted. I felt something afoot.

January 1553
Near Hatfield House Hertfordshire

I was right, I had been outwitted. John Dudley sent me away from court directly after the holiday. And with Amy settled in Somerset, I was basically rendered homeless in London. I retreated to Hatfield to lick my wounds. I had to get better at this game of intrigue if I were to ever gain the crown.

Not two days after I arrived at Hatfield, I got word that Edward was indeed very ill, and I was requested at his side.

I instantly had Kat repack my belongs, but before we had exited for the carriage, the door was opened, and a courier was presented to me. This courier directly handed me a letter. Upon opening it, I read:

My lady princess,

Do not come to Whitehall. There are plots afoot that you cannot be connected with.

W. C.

William's letter held no greeting, which was our signal that the message was of dire import. Kat paid the courier a silver coin. I knew enough about my good friend's ability to evade danger to take this warning seriously.

After I commanded the travel plans to cease, Kat asked, "what is all this about, my lady?"

"I am uncertain Kat, only Sir William fears for my safety." Disappointed, I looked at the letter again. "It will take months to again get permission from the court to see Edward. He is indeed very sick; I know this from Sir William. I fear for him, Kat. I am sure he needs me. However, there seems to be some plotting afoot that I need to stay clear of." I handed the letter to her and continued, "Curse the court and Lord Dudley!"

Kat read the letter and said, "I do not understand it either, but Sir William has shown himself to be a very astute correspondent and rather protective of you, so I am glad you listen to what he suggests."

I dressed warmly and took Larkin out for a ride. There was much to think on, and I needed peace and my horse to accomplish the job.

That night I dreamt of my dear brother. I saw him in his death bed, and I knew I would not see him on this earth again.

May 1553
Hatfield house, Hertfordshire

My life seemed to be falling apart. I had not heard from Robert in over six months and, though I petitioned Lord John Dudley weekly, he would not allow me to come to London and see my brother. I sat writing another letter.

Lord Dudley,

I plead with you to let me visit Edward. It has been many long months since I have been with him and I feel he needs his family now. This is the thirtieth letter I have sent, with barely the courtesy of a reply. Please send me word that I may come. It is very wicked of you to keep me from his side. I beg of you to allow me to give him comfort.

Best Regards,
Elizabeth

The letter was sealed and sent, but no sooner had I hastened the courier out, then another appeared at my door bearing a letter with two seals. It was from William, of course.

My lady princess,

Lord Dudley will have his son, Lord Guildford, married to Lady Jane Grey before the month is gone. The king is worse every day and cannot sleep without a tonic. Word has leaked about his majesty the king's final document; he is calling it 'The Device'. It is an agreement of parliament that no woman shall have the throne of England. Thus, Lord Dudley's haste in getting Lady Jane married. At present, no parliamentary act has been signed but I fear that it will not matter.

The king asks for you daily, I think he knows he himself has made it impossible for you to visit. I beg you to stay where you are. Those that want the Tudor line to cease are willing to do anything.

I have some other news that I know you will find highly disturbing. I have cut ties with Lord Robert Dudley, for he is in the service of his father and is in fact the main enforcer of all his father's plots. I fear for your friend greatly should things go amiss with the inevitable coup.

I know that you miss your brother, but you cannot help but see how dangerous an air infects the royal court at present. My advice to you would be to stay away.

With concern,
W.C.

Shock permeated through my body. What was Robert's game? I had to believe it was to help me. I could not see him do anything else.

Also, it seemed so long ago that the two of us had speculated on what his father would do, what the council would do, in order to force Mary and myself out. Speculation was one thing, but now there was proof. The council's treasonous acts would make all those fears from before come to pass, and I could do nothing. How dare they. How dare all of them.

I knew that it was only a few lines on a piece of paper that declared Mary and I's place in the line of succession, but they were also the wishes a dying king which parliament ratified into law. There was a proper order to things here in England. I was a princess by birth and by law!

Furthermore, the method of secession was law.

How dare these men change father's wishes! Ultimately it would be Edward who saw the deed done, but how much pressure was he truly under? He needed help. I unfolded the letter again to read its words once more. This time the bit about Jane caught my attention.

"There is no way Jane wants this, she is not that foolish," I whispered to myself. *This is all treasonous.* Mary would have none of it. She had a very strong backing. She had Spain on her side and Rome. She had an army of her own and John Dudley was foolish to trifle with that.

I had to choose a side. I did not want Mary to be queen, but I understood that it was her and I, or neither of us. So, I had to choose her. I had to help her.

I knew what that meant though. I'd had enough dreams of Mary, drenched in blood. I knew what she would do. The image of Jane, Lord Dudley, all the council and... Robert, hanged for treason under a Queen Mary filled my mind. "Oh God in heaven!" I cried out and tears of anger and sorrow flooded down my cheeks. If Robert's involvement was made known to Mary once she had the crown--and she would have the crown--she would certainly have his head for it, just as she would have his father's and all the Protestant rebels... Jane's too, the poor girl.

I would have to save them, all of them if I could. If not, I would have to do everything in my power to save Robert from Mary. I thought back on my dream, Mary's hand with blood dripping from her nails. Mary always had long, pointed nails. I teased her that filing her nails with a rock was really what she did while at her prayer bench. It did not seem like a funny joke now.

～

Just as William told me, on the twenty-first day of May, Lady Jane Grey was married to none other than Lord Guildford Dudley, Robert's brother. So much of Guildford's involvement at court made sense with this wedding.

I was not invited, though Jane was my cousin. In truth, the wedding took place so quickly after the engagement that I *could not* have come.

This told me one thing. Edward was dying and he was doing so quickly.

June 1553

Hatfield House, Hertfordshire

I received two letters at once. I opened the one with the seal of Lord John Dudley upon it first.

My Lady Elizabeth,

I am happy to tell you that we would be honored to receive you at court. In fact, the king sends word that he will expect you within the week. He is gravely ill and needs his family about him.

Lord John Dudley

I was overjoyed but very scared for my brother. Yet I quelled my happiness until I read the letter from William.
In my haste to see what it said, I ripped the paper.

My lady princess,

I am loath to tell you this, but your brother is on his death bed. He coughs up nothing but black tar and I fear that he has given up, he is so tired of his illness. I do not think it will be long. Lord Dudley has brought Lady Jane and Lord Guildford to Greenwich and they wait the sad occasion.

Also, the king has signed The Device and parliament is acting quickly to get it ratified and enforced as law. I read it and it declares all we feared for you and your sister.

Do not come here for I fear for your life. Hide if you can, for, I believe that there will be bloodshed before this is over.

> *Your faithful servant,*
> *W.C.*

Anger and disappointment almost clouded out the sadness I felt for my sweet brother. What he must have gone through…to write such a vile lie into law…to betray us, his sisters, and in such a way. It was reprehensible, for without our position, who were we in the eyes of the people… of the gentry… of the court?

"What have the letters to say, my lady?" Kat asked absentmindedly as she worked her needle.

The note went into the fire just as all notes of this nature. "Sir William is convinced that Lord Dudley will hold me captive until Edward expires, so that I will not make any trouble when he tries to put Jane on the throne." I would not give Robert away, even to Kat.

"Heaven forbid!" Kat said in a strangled voice.

"Yes, I am afraid for Mary. I must get word to her, for they surely will kill her. She is too supported by the populous to be conveniently deposed."

"They would not dare, my lady. The people will cause an upheaval should they attempt a coup, and though she is horrid to you, I would join them. She is the rightful queen, no matter her religion." Kat understood most of the problems facing our country, but she failed to acknowledge that the council would actually kill any of the royal line just to get a Protestant on the throne.

They would, and Edward would help them if he could. "Yes Kat, I know. Mary should be queen, but also… I fear."

I'd had more dreams. Only a fortnight ago I had dreamt I saw fire and heard screams and I saw Mary's face in the midst of the horror. I knew instantly that Mary would tear the country end from end. I did not want any harm to come to my sister, but I would give up my status as princess only to prevent the terror I beheld in that dream.

I knew that Edward was doing all he could to stop a catholic from gaining the throne upon his death. The words of his letter to me, which came just yesterday, came to my mind.

"My beloved Elizabeth, take nothing that shall happen in the next few months as an insult to you, I beg of you to heed me. I will see that the financial stipulations in father's will are honored. I only wish to preserve my life's work and the work of our father in his final years."

I, of course, knew what this had to mean, for William had warned me months ago that it would come to this. Edward did not know what he was talking of, for if he could take us out of the will, then the next king could take our inheritance as well, a new council could reduce Mary and me to poverty in a fortnight.

I went straight to my writing desk.

My dearest sister,

I hope you are in good health. I write to plead with you to forgo any trips into London. If you did not know, Edward is extremely sick, and I have received word that there is a plot to capture you in order to keep you from the throne should Edward die. My source is remarkably trustworthy, and I fear exceedingly for your life. Make haste please and leave Hunsdon. You and your guard are welcome at Hatfield that we might protect ourselves together, yet I think it wiser for you to go elsewhere and hide yourself.

I pray that this will reach you in time. God be with you, my sister, and protect you from any evil that may trespass.

I pray for the soul of our dearest Edward as well.

With Love,
Elizabeth

    I sent for a courier and soon the letter was off with great haste. I had done my duty and I hoped that she, as queen, would do her duty to me and to the people of England. As for me, there was only one way to deal with this. I would have to utilize all the hours of drama I had in school and put on one of the best shows of my life.

July 1553
Hatfield House, Hertfordshire

I had come up with a scheme I hoped would help me stay away from court in this troubled time, and had spread it profusely to the masses. I lay in my 'sick bed' when I first officially received the news of my brother's death. First from Master Parry and then a letter from William. But on the day of my brother's death I did not have to pretend. I had had horrid dreams all night and when I woke, I knew what had transpired.

Master Parry said, as he handed me a letter, "my lady, I am so sorry that you are so ill at this terribly tragic time. I am also so sorry to tell you this, but your brother the king is dead, my lady. Long live Queen Jane." His voice was quiet and mournful.

I took Kat's hand in one of mine and my sheet in the other as tears filled my eyes and spilled down my face. I wiped them with the sheet. "Thank you, Master Parry, for your haste. I must be alone now. Leave me, please."

He did leave and I sat with my ladies, not wanting to open the paper. Eventually I did.

My lady princess,

I am sure that you know by now, your brother has passed from this world. Lord Robert Dudley and a royal guard were sent to arrest Mary; he desired I send his dearest affection in case the worst should

happen. I do not fully trust the man, but I am cognizant of the peril he is
in should he fail, and am thus obliged to repeat his words to you.

    I am certain that Lady Jane will be declared queen very soon,
for I know your brother made some last-minute changes to his Device,
making it possible for that lady to hold the position.

    I am sorry that you are unwell. I must say that I hope your 'sick-
ness' keeps you out of court for at least a while longer, for the bloodbath
is about to begin.

    Yours etc.
    W.C.

I could not believe it. Edward was dead. I wiped at my eyes again
and again, the tears seemed to not want to stop. I thought I had prepared
myself, but it was not enough. Can one never be prepared for the death
of a loved one? I found more than the news of Edward disturbing though,
and I tried to think through the other information as well. What was
Robert thinking? How in the world did he expect to take Mary down? I
myself had warned her and therefore put her out of harm's way. What did
this mean for Robert?

    I felt numb with sorrow and fear.

T he next thing I knew I had received a letter from Mary and yet
another from William.

    My dear sister,

    Thank you so much for your warning letter, it was most timely.
Because of it, I was able to get away from the traitors sent to capture me.
I have proclaimed myself queen and am gathering a force here in

Kenninghall, and plan to march on London within the fortnight. I am well received and have the support of the people and arms men here, and many join our ranks every moment.

I write to ask you also to join me as I ride into London. I feel you have already cast your lot with me and would appreciate your support; moreover, I call for it as your queen. I know you have the people's love and feel that with you at my side, not even Lord Dudley can stop us from our birthright.

Rest assured, my sister, that your loyalty in this matter will not be forgotten.

Affectionately,
Mary R
Queen of England

I was not impressed with how she lumped us together now that she felt I could be of use to her. Though I did see how this all was working for my advantage. I quickly opened William's letter to see what he had to say.

My lady princess,

It is but four days after your brother's death and Jane has declared herself Queen. She has set herself up in the Tower. Lord Dudley is at her side, but I think that she will send him off to fight Mary and help capture her. With your sister unaccounted for, Lady Jane's position is weak at best. As soon as he is gone, I plan on starting an intrigue against him.

I fear the part that I must play in all of this, for your brother the late king forced me to sign his Device. I did not desire to do so for you know that I am very strictly loyal to particular members of your family. Still, I do not desire to see Lady Jane on the throne, despite her Protestant inclination.

I loathe having to say these words and hope you will not begrudge me this favor, but I fear I will soon be a desperate man and I hope that our acquaintance may offer me some security.

Furthermore, I do not know what position I will be in to continue communication, so forgive me if this is the last you hear from me and God bless you.

> *Your faithful servant,*
> *William C.*

Poor William, what he must be suffering? It seemed that there would be several people I would need to take responsibility for should Mary gain the throne. I began to see Jane in a different light. It did not take much to make my decision. Blessed William helped me do so as he always did. I sat to write two letters of response.

Sir,

Please make yourself easy, I will see to everything. You will have to do what you must, but so will I. You have my support.

> *Your friend,*
> *E.*

Majesty,

Thank the Lord that all is going well there. I will tell you I have news that Jane is not supported here. The council sits in support of her and thinks that they are all powerful and thus have nothing to fear from you. Yet everyone around me is on your side. Also, I know that they are sending John Dudley who, you well know, is a general of great deference, to come capture you so be on your guard.

I will ride with you at any time. I of course am with you and at your command, my queen.

With love and support,
Elizabeth

I sent both letters out and quickly. There was much thinking to do and I could not pace around the house while doing so.

Robert and William, how would I save them? How could I even gain Mary's ear or trust? I had not openly proclaimed myself a Protestant. I did not have to. It was how I was raised, but I had not denied Rome anything nor fought it, so I found myself open to several possibilities.

I had a headache, but there was so much to think on. I needed the air in my face and sky up above me and the earth moving beneath me, but I still had a part to play, so I pulled the light of my grandmothers to me and all their knowledge came with it.

My mind wandered in and out of possibilities and with a few minutes, I knew what I must do.

The Tower lay just ahead of us as the crowds pressed around the open carriage. The shouting had begun to hurt my ears. I sat at Mary's side as she waved to the crowd and touched them when she could. She was all deference and modesty. I thought she might have taken a page from my book of plays, for her act was superbly... humble.

The last few days had flown by as a leaf in a whirlwind. Lord Dudley had quickly surrendered and declared Mary queen when he saw the force she had gathered. He now traveled at the back of our company as a prisoner. I did not know what Mary would do to him, but I was sure that my beloved Robert would lose his father within the week.

We reached the Tower and Mary swept into the grand entryway accompanied by me and one hundred of her guard. All had abandoned Jane, thus there was no bloodshed, thank the Lord. Within the hour upon being received, the entire council, Jane, and Guildford stood before Mary. The council declared her the queen, of course, and then it was time to see what she would do.

"I call for the imprisonment of Lord John Dudley, Guildford Dudley, and the Lady Jane Grey. Take them to the Tower prison at once." I saw that none of the council would stop her. At this point they all feared for their lives.

Jane cried out once, "have mercy, cousin. I was coerced. I was forced. Have mercy..." But the guard had taken them already and had shut her cries behind a door.

Mary straightened her dress and looked at the rest of the council. "You are all under house arrest. I will investigate whom of you I can trust and whom I cannot. Until then, you will not leave. I will also be appointing new members, starting with Lord Thomas Howard and Cardinal Steven Gardiner, both of which are imprisoned here, I believe." Someone nodded, and Mary continued, "you," she pointed at a nearby guard, "go and fetch them." The man did as she told him.

On and on it went, until Mary had established her supremacy and all were bowing and scraping at her feet. Later, I saw William Cecil. After nodding to me, he petitioned the queen to speak with her in private. I knew what he must do now, he must betray every single member of the council in order to save his own life. So, I did what I could to help. I surrounded myself with light, looked at Mary and threw the words I needed as hard as I could. *This man is useful. He is a loyal supporter of the Tudor line. Give him a chance to prove himself.* I sent the light to Mary and watched as it affected her, and she gave William consent to speak with her.

Several hours later, a list of arrests was published, and I smiled, knowing that William had proven his worth. I next saw him hurrying toward the chapel where I learned he attended an impromptu mass and asked for forgiveness for his bout of Protestantism. I was not pleased, but knew I would be next, so I did not judge. We both would do what we must to survive, for we knew Mary would have her way.

September 1553
Richmond Palace, London

Mary summoned me to her thrown room, which was a very bad sign. She sat there, the as-of-yet uncrowned queen regnant of England. I was uncertain why I was here, but I waited as Mary looked me up and down. Finally, she spoke, "Sister, you have not attended mass with me as I have asked. Why is this?"

Instantly, all was made known unto me. Mary would mark her reign with strict religious regulations, and she would start humbling this nation by bringing me in line. I looked around. There were hundreds of people in the chamber, each one with their eyes on me. Oh yes, Mary wanted a show, she wanted me to kneel before her and forsake all. I surrounded myself with light but knew that it would be almost impossible to use with so many people around; and if I did use it, I would have to be so delicate that Mary's strong mind would probably never be influenced. I must fend for myself. I would do what it took for I still had not found a way to save Robert.

"I have not been well, my queen. I fear the stress of these last few months have taken a heavy toll upon me and I have been in bed more often than I would like to admit in front of so many," I said quietly. I had played this card so many times that I did not think Mary would buy it, so I thought quickly of some other excuse.

I was wrong, though. Mary's face instantly softened, and she stood and came to me. However, before she could say anything, Stephen Gardiner intercepted her. "Your majesty, I do not see how this can be born. She is well enough now, let her go and worship with us at this moment." He turned to me with a hateful look in his eye. "Unless she is deceiving and manipulating us all."

I was sure that the shock at his words registered on my face. He had not forgotten my earlier shame and wrongdoings; he had not overlooked my Protestant upbringing. He was my enemy, and he was the bee in Mary's ear, provoking her to anger.

I had no issue with going to mass, except it was dreadfully boring and I did not know if I remembered when to stand or sit or sing or quote. I realized that this was my next plan.

Mary looked at me and spoke, "well, I can see that you are shocked at his accusations, and that only leads me to believe it to be true." She sighed heavily and moved away from me. "What is to be done with you, then? If you have truly been refusing to obey me, there must be some punishment."

My anger was hot. How dare all of these people. I stood proudly before my sister and looked her in the face. "My good queen, I beg you to consider what you are saying. I am your sister and a princess of England. Should our brother have punished you for not submitting to his will? You did not stop your priest performing mass in your chapels even after the law against such was ratified. I do not think you should punish me for being obedient to what I know, for I know that to be a virtue you value."

"You see, my queen, how haughty and defiant she is. She admits that she was pretending and thus she is a liar also."

"I said nothing of the kind."

"Silence!" Mary said loudly. She looked at me and I could see the logical wheels of her head turning.

It was time to humble myself. I had stood up to her and let her know who I was and that I would not be treated thus, and now it was time to show her that I was also a subject.

I went to my knees and forced tears to come to my eyes, though I did not tremble, sniffle or blather.

"I beg mercy, my queen. I have not been raised as you. This sudden change has me confused. There are real questions that need to be answered and I know not the answers to them. I have... *had* a brother and a beloved father who told me I must worship one way, or I am a traitor and a blasphemer. Now you have the throne and you and your counselors tell me that I must change all my traditions in a blink of an eye, or I am a traitor and a blasphemer. Tell me, sister, who is right, and I will believe you. I only wish to serve you; you must see that."

Mary's heart was softened. "Of course you are confused, my sister." She did come to me then. "But we will educate you in what is right and proper." She turned to Gardiner. "Will we not, my lords?" Eventually they nodded grudgingly.

Yes, this was what was needed. It would not be so bad to learn more about Catholicism. "Thank you, my queen." I wiped the tears from my face and looked up at her. "Let me learn so that I may go in the right way."

She smiled down on me and I could see the joy that she found in 'saving my soul.' Moreover, I saw that I was out of danger.

I took advantage of her closeness to pull my power to me and whisper in her ear. Robert had been captured and imprisoned shortly after she arrived triumphant in London. I hated to think of him in the Tower, but I would do what I could. "Robert Dudley is also one whose soul can be saved. Save him!" I pushed the light toward her hard and hoped it helped.

October 1553
Hampton Court, London

Mary was crowned England's first Queen regnant. As a woman, she could not hold the power of the crown, only the right to it, which she would pass to her husband when she married. Making *him* king and her, *his* queen. Regardless, it was a pompous ceremony, but everything with Mary seemed pompous. The lady Anna of Cleves, my father's only surviving wife, attended, and it was lovely to see her after such a long absence.

Mary invited me to stay and insisted that I attend mass with her. I did not argue, and I spent an obscene amount of time on my bench, praying that God would help me save Robert and myself from Mary's reign. She planned on trying every last one of the Dudleys for high treason and had already tried and executed Lord John Dudley. She had spared Jane and Guildford in a benevolent act that spoke to all who did not know of her magnanimous character.

The truth was I had used my power on Mary for Jane's sake. Jane was sorely used and did not deserve to die for her crimes, she was but seventeen and completely controlled by the council. If Mary was not going to hang the old council, she should not do so to Jane.

I did not know what would happen at the trial, and I could not control that outcome. I would not be there, and I could not control so many minds at once if I were. I only hoped that all would be well with her and quieted my conscious by doing all I could with Mary.

I had also used my power again on Mary concerning Robert's predicament, but her anger and hatred toward him and his family was too great. She had John killed quickly, and all I accomplished was to save Robert from the headsmen's block in quick succession after his father.

At least William was safe for the moment. Mary had sent him on some diplomatic mission already. And though I knew that was code for '*I do not completely trust you, so I am going to send you off to some unknown corner of the world,*' I knew that she would soon see his uses.

I felt so responsible for these people and whispered power-filled words to Mary every moment I could. I knew that in my mind I was taking responsibility for the life of all my friends, and I saw the danger of it, for too many elements were completely out of my control. I felt sad and angry often, proving this was too great a burden for me to bear. Still, I did try.

November 1553
Whitehall Palace, London

I sat trembling in my room. William told me the news a few days ago, but now I sat with a letter in my hand and the seal was that of the house of Dudley. I fought with myself, as tears raged down my cheeks. Finally, I wiped my eyes and cracked the seal.

My dearest Elizabeth,

I am able to write to my family and inform them that I have been convicted as a traitor and will be beheaded. The court has only now just made the ruling, and Queen Mary the sentence. I am writing to you to tell you goodbye.

Do not be angry, my love, I knew what I was doing as I was doing it. In truth, it could not be helped. Father, God rest his soul, was doing what he could to help himself and I was doing what I could to help you. I cannot say more, but know that your dream and your birthright were all I thought of.

I do not know when the deed shall be done, so I will take this chance to tell you how I feel. My darling, I am so excruciatingly sorry for our argument. I did not know what to say. I did not know how to act. I felt pulled in two directions and though I love only you, I felt that you needed to re-choose me. Re-choose the life we promised to one another. I sensed you felt trapped and I never wanted that for you.

I did my best to give you freedom. I did my best to love you and help you from afar. I honored my promises to you and that is all I can take with me now. Please forgive me if you feel I have not done as I should. Please forgive me for any hurt that has transpired these last years. Know that to my dying day, I was on your side.

Elizabeth, your face is all I see. I will die with you in my heart and on my mind. I love you more than life. We have had all we could ask for. How many people get to have so much time with the love of their life? Not many I dare say. Know that as I sit here in the Tower, my mind will be running through all of our happiest memories and know that those memories will keep me warm and contented.

I love you. I love you. I love you. Forever.

Your Robin

The letter dropped from my hand and hit the carpet with a soft thump. This was not possible. Without thought, without decision, I flung myself out of the room and toward the stables.

Galloping Scooter as fast as he would go, I reached the Tower in excellent time and ran to find Mary. She could not see me. Though I pleaded and cried, they would not let me see her but led me to a room where I could wait to be seen.

I could not tolerate this treatment. I could not comprehend what was happening. I paced up and down the room and found that my mind felt on the point of bursting. What could I do? I knew exactly what I needed to do, but would the situation permit it? And I instantly knew the answer to that question. It did not matter. This was the entire reason I had power. For good. Robert was good. I would not let Robert die.

After what seemed like the longest afternoon of my life, someone finally brought me to Mary. I found her sitting in her throne room looking the fearsome queen she was. I burst through the door feeling every bit like Esther from the bible; however, I did not have a whole nation of people fasting and praying for my success.

The instant I entered, I knew that I was in very real danger.

"What is the meaning of this, Elizabeth?" The look on her face was not at all pleasant and her guards had crossed to me and were about to pull me back. However, I took care of them with a thought and a bit of light. Then I quickly assessed the room and counted only a dozen or so courtiers and council members present.

I noticed Stephen Gardiner and Simon Renard near her side. They made me wince for some reason, but I did not have time to analyze the feeling, for Mary was going on. "Just because you are my sister..." I did not listen, pulling a dozen large orbs together as I said the words of the manipulation so quietly that none could hear but those guards right next to me. You will not kill Robert Dudley. You will not harm him in any way. As I walked forward, toward Mary, I sent several orbs repeating that same manipulation. The other manipulations I sent to the crowd of people were: you do not recall exactly how I now stand before you, but you are happy to see me. I was scared and had not had occasion to use my power for quite some time, and so I pushed the orbs harder than I needed.

As a result, by the time I was at Mary's side she shook her head forcefully, and then confused eyes focused on my face. I sent one more orb to her. You are happy to see me and are anxious to calm my fears. Then I said, "Forgive me, my queen, I only just heard the news that the trial of my friend Robert Dudley was concluded. I was anxious to hear your sentence."

"Of course, my dear," she said, smiling warmly at me. "I know how you are worried for your friend. He has committed treason, Elizabeth, and you know the punishment for that crime as well as any should." I gasped, and she went on quickly. "However, be comforted for his part was small and, in the end, I shall pardon him, for I understand that he has been only following his father's wishes, and was under duress of some kind. Truly he is inconsequential. I, of all people, understand how difficult it can be to make sure a father's wishes are obeyed." There was a murmur of agreeance from those in attendance. "But here, I stand in front of all these witnesses and promise you that he will not be harmed in any way. I only wish to punish him by keeping him in the Tower until he understands fully the depth of his wrongs and he forsakes his sacrilege. I will not kill him." She smiled around the room, "I cannot kill everyone who acted against me, or there would be not many in this room still alive." She fixed her gaze pointedly on several individuals, but I did not care about that. I only waited for her to finish her speech. "I fear the Lord would frown on so much bloodshed, for it really is a simple matter of pride. Only if I must fight and draw blood in a battle sanctioned by God himself, would I not be held accountable." She dry-washed her hands expressively and continued, "No... death is not the answer for such crimes as his, a firm hand and harsh punishment is, and that is all Lord Dudley will receive."

Mary took my hands and I nodded to her counselors, who looked to be in agreeance with the queen. "Thank you, Mary, my queen, you are so good in your heart. I have no doubt that we all do not deserve you." I only hoped that her 'goodness' would last. Mary had a strong mind and she had overcome my manipulations before, so I was determined to stay close to her and watch and listen. Although it did seem as though she had planned this from the start, and I could see the wisdom in it.

Mary's face brightened. "I am happy you are here. For I have something to show you, something perhaps only a sister can help with."

As we walked, I wondered that I should not have manipulated her each time I saw her, for she was highly pleasant and seemed truly happy to see me. She prattled along about affairs of state, and once we neared the royal bedchambers, she began a new conversation. "So, the council is urging me to marry as soon as possible, for I must bear a son. I have had many interesting offers, but have not found anything thus far pleasing, until a letter arrived from my cousin, Charles. He offers Philip to me. I know that an alliance with the Spanish would make the French insane. Henri might just leap across the channel in anger. Perhaps then he would regret... oh, never mind."

I wondered at Mary's slip. Had there been an agreement of some sort between Henri and herself? It did not matter, a marriage with Spain would be a disaster. "Have you not found a single Englishman to your liking, my queen?"

She laughed. "You sound like Gardiner and Renard, they cannot believe it possible. There are plenty of pleasing Englishmen who would never look at me twice, except now that I am the queen they clamor for my hand. Truthfully, there is but one that would do, but he is our cousin and really a very dear friend. I just do not know if that is what I want to do."

"Which cousin?" I knew of course.

"Edward Courtenay. I have made him Earl of Devon. He is very handsome, yet there are some fundamental differences between us, which I find very hard. He is Protestant. I think marrying him would send a message that I am willing to deal kindly with that movement, and in truth, I am not!" She took a long deep breath and then continued. "Moreover, I long to do all that my mother… could not." She glanced at me out of the corner of her eyes and finished. "I long for Spain and England to be friends again. I would like to deal with my cousins there."

I wanted to say, 'But Mary, as queen, you must not do what you want in marriage, you must do what is best for country and people.' However, I did not. I only thought of this for myself and knew that if in her place, I would never take my own advice. "I see. Does Philip share your passion for religion?"

"Yes, as far as I can tell, they are much stricter with the Protestant movement in Spain." Her eyebrows furrowed for a moment.

"He is a man of war, then?"

"No more than most." She smiled, but again the eyes held concern.

"Is he opposed to living in England?"

"I do not think so, how could he be? He is not the king of anything at present and here, he would be."

That was the other thing I worried about and was hoping to make her see. Having a husband would lessen her so much to the people and the council. He would be king, and she would have to do as he said. I would much rather rule myself and do what my conscious dictated me to do with the country. She would be a figurehead at best, when, at present, she was not. However, that would still be true with an English husband... king, yet at least the people would know that an Englishman would have their best interest in his heart, and that he would protect them from all countries. "And what if we were to war with Spain? What side would he be on?"

"Oh, Elizabeth, the council hammers these questions at me night and day. Here," she said and opened a door. "I wanted to show you the portrait Charles sent."

Before me stood a full-sized canvas of Philip himself. "He is very good looking."

Mary was bouncing childishly. "Is he not! I cannot help but have my eyes on this portrait for hours of the day."

I looked over at her and saw that she fancied herself in love with this man. There would be no good telling her anything bad about the situation, for she would not listen. She was a thirty-seven-year-old virgin, she needed a man in her life. I had a feeling in my gut that it would be her undoing, but I also knew that there was nothing I could do but separate myself from the whole disaster. "Yes, sister, I think he will do just fine. He is very handsome, and he seems to have won you over in every particular. So, I am very happy for you. When will the marriage take place?"

"Oh, I have only just received the offer and I am in deep conversations with the council about it every day. They are being stubborn, but I am determined to write Charles this week and tell him we must start discussing the terms of the marriage treaty."

I took a chance and went to her. Clasping her hands in mine, I said, "I am very happy for you. I know you have waited so patiently for so long. You are a very good woman and deserve the very best of men." I decided that I would later seek out William Cecil; I needed a crafty mind to discuss this matter with. I hoped it was my personal trepidations, and that I was mistaken about the mood of the people. For if I was not mistaken, Mary was indeed boiling a kettle of water that I feared she would be doused in.

Mary blushed profusely. "Thank you, sister." She said sincerely and looked at me with quizzical eyes. "Tell me, how go your catholic lessons?"

"They are going well." I did not want to go here, for I knew that it would be hard for me to get out of telling her how very much I disagreed with what was being taught.

"Tell me what you are thinking, for I can see your mind working."

I coughed and smiled at her. "Well, I think that the idea of the pope standing in place of Christ on the earth is an interesting difference. I have always believed men to be so flawed that it is almost impossible to think one could stand as Christ on the earth. Not even Peter the apostle did that. However, the idea of someone leading the church in the name of Christ resonates with my spirit greatly."

Mary nodded and smiled, though her forehead wrinkled as if she were trying to decide whether I was admitting that I was converted, or if I was only dancing around the issue. I went on. "I do wonder if none of us do quite enough good. The thought that certain works along with faith in Christ bring salvation is very good, I think. I have always believed that a person truly converted to Christ would do His works in everyday life. That he would become like Christ in all ways possible naturally by obeying the commandments. That salvation, real honest recognized salvation, changes the man from the natural form to the godly one, and thus his actions must be different. Do you not think so, my queen?"

Mary was astounded. She clearly did not know what to say. "Yes, the seven sacraments are essential."

I foolishly went on, "I only see a major flaw in the thought that one cannot read from the bible and gain spiritual understanding for themselves. I believe that life and experiences can help anyone understand the words of the Lord, for He uses practical analogies, and was He not talking to the simplest of people? Was it not the learned men who rejected him?"

Instantly, I knew that I had gone too far. "That is quite enough, Elizabeth! I will not have your vile rhetoric in my ears a moment longer. You spoke so kindly a moment ago, and then you weld your chains of blasphemy and confusion around me, and I am finished. You will leave me at once and I will not see you again until you have repented of your devilish thoughts and submitted to me and to Rome. I will have submission, Elizabeth, and I grow tired of waiting."

With that, she pointed her finger at me, and I was forced to walk away from her.

Surprised by her sudden outburst, I did as she bade, but it would prove to be a costly mistake.

December 1553
Durham Palace, London

Mary was truly angry with me and had exiled me from court in earnest. Without the help of William—heaven knows where Mary had sent that man now—I was lost to most political news, for I had very few friends in Mary's court.

Over the next few weeks I only heard from my casual informants that Robert was still in the Tower. Mary was keeping her word though she was angry with me. I hoped that I had not spurred her onward in her quest, for by the end of the month not only had Mary abolished Edward's religious laws, but she had announced her marriage to Philip of Spain. It seemed that all of my fears were about to come true.

Before the New Year arrived, I had received letters informing me that Jane's father was secretly talking with anyone who would listen, trying to stir up revolt against Mary. After Mary's recent actions, some were in favor of putting his daughter on the throne once more. I quickly penned him a letter telling him if there was one sure way to see his daughter killed, and soon, it was to continue his foolishness. Mary would not allow a usurper with any power to live one day longer than necessary.

He did not respond, but I did receive a very strange letter from someone I had never met in my life. Kat brought it in to me several days before the first of January.

"This just came addressed to Sir John, and he thought you might be interested in its contents."

I took the letter and read.

Lord Ashley,

I know we have met but on a rare occasion, but I am writing to you for I know that you are over my cousin, the princess Elizabeth's, household. I would be so obliged if you would tell me, has she any suitors? I am interested in beginning some negotiations in that regard and wondered if I could trespass on her time next Sunday at teatime.

Please arrange a meeting and I will also discuss this business with yourself.

Best regards
Edward Courtenay
Earl of Devon

I received letters containing marriage propositions all the time; it was normal for one of my status. Most were only inquiries of this sort, yet this came from someone who just recently courted my sister the queen, so it seemed shocking.

"Sir John is right, Kat, I am very interested in this letter." I folded it up and looked to her. Her face held a strange expression which I attempted to alleviate. "Of course, I will not even discuss this matter with him. He only just was turned down by Mary, and that does not speak highly of his ambitions, now does it?"

Her face softened. "It does not indeed, my lady." She said it with a bit of pretense. I suspected that she and John knew why this letter would be of importance to me, and that was why he had Kat bring it.

"Tell your husband that he outdoes himself in my service. However, I would like him to let my cousin down easily, for he has just had a heartbreak and I would not want to send him into the deep abyss of crushed suitors."

Kat laughed, "yes, how will his heart ever get over such sadness. Two loves lost and all in the work of a few weeks' time."

"I say, Kat, you left out the most important part. Two royal loves lost." We both had a good laugh at my cousin's expense.

I did not want to go back to Ashridge, for I wanted to stay near Robert and Mary so that I could make sure all went well there. However, when January came, so did the word of rebellion in the country. I feared that Hatfield might be the safest place, and so I began preparing my household for the move. It was as I was doing such, that Sir John entered with a thick parchment in his hands and a very worried look on his face. It was his habit to read all my unsolicited letters and I did not mind it. More often than not, he took care of the things that I was loathe to even think of.

"What is it, John? You look as if you have seen death."

"I fear, my lady, that I…" He handed me the letter. "Here, a man by the name of Lord Russell brought this not a half an hour past," he said uncomfortably, and bowed his way out of the room.

However, when I turned it over, the seal had not been broken. I opened the paper with trembling hands and prayed that it held nothing of Robert in its lines.

My Lady Princess,

I am well into plans of rebellion against your sister, the queen. Her marriage to the Spanish prince will ruin us. Shall we allow England to be overrun with foreigners and foreign policy and foreign wars? I dare say we shall not!

Furthermore, the tide of the land is no longer sympathetic to Catholicism. We are a Protestant country now and we need a Protestant ruler.

I am very bold with you, my lady, because I hope and pray that you will be that ruler. When I and my army have taken the Catholic witch off the throne, we will put you on it, if you are willing. We begin our march within the fortnight, so if you are opposed to this plan, do what you must;

however, if you are for the plan, gather forces of your own. I am certain you will see us coming.

Thomas Wyatt

P.S. For your personal safety, I would love to offer you protection, should you want to move to a more secure house, such as Donnington. I am at your disposal.

Before the words were completely in my mind, I threw the paper into the fire. Heaven forbid! What could be done? What was I to do? I collapsed into a chair and began to consider.

Surrounding myself with the power, my thoughts cleared, and peace came. I knew in my heart that I could not go against Mary, though it was a very tempting notion. I feared exceedingly all that she would do to the kingdom. I had seen in my dreams what would happen and how so many would die. This thought was especially poignant since the last I saw her, she had spoken of blood on her hands.

Nevertheless, I could do nothing to take her down. It would not be right; I knew it in my soul. Joining myself with Thomas Wyatt was out of the question. The operative dilemma now was, what do I do with this new information? I could not simply tell Mary that a rebel had contacted me; she would instantly see me for what I was. I was her only potential successor... for now, at least. She knew the people were sympathetic toward me, for she had heard them calling my name as we came triumphantly into London. I definitely did not need to draw attention to myself in that light.

Moreover, Mary would have to see the tide that the nation was going. There were too many powerful Protestants about and if they wanted a coup d'état, I would be their natural choice for ruler.

Though I had not declared myself an absolute proponent for the Protestant cause, it was known that my father had set up my household with Protestant tutors and servants, and had insisted my church devotion be in the Protestant tradition. I was labeled before having made the decision for myself. The problem at present was that I was labeled to oppose Mary.

That was it. I could not openly be a part of this information or plot at all. My name could not be connected, or I would be at the Tower faster than Robert had been. And though Mary may resist trying me, I knew two men who would not. Gardiner and Renard. They had both suffered personally at the hands of Protestants and thus were haters, and I, to them, was just that. One of their persecutors, and they would never see me as anything else.

I could do nothing and that was my only option.

I called my servant, William St. Loe, to me. The small balding man entered the room hesitantly. "Master St. Loe, I would ask you to deliver a message for me."

He held out his hand, his face a little confused. "As you wish, my lady princess."

I smiled at him, "thank you, but I will not be writing it down. It is of a sensitive nature and I would have you memorize it."

Now he understood, for he was of quick wit and very loyal to the Protestant cause. "Yes, my lady."

"I would wish you to say, 'Thank you, sir, for your good will, and I will do only as I should see cause. If you see me, you see me.'" I smiled again and hoped it was cryptic enough. Then I asked him to repeat it. Once he had, I said, "the message is to go to Lord Thomas Wyatt." The man's eye lit up. "I will have you ride the fastest horse, and I wish you to not be deterred for any reason. Please leave at once and tell no one."

"Of course, my lady, thank you." And he bowed himself out.

I hoped that that would take care of several sensitive matters, yet would not promise anything to the recipient.

I next called John and Master Parry to my study. "Sirs, I call you here to tell you I feel we might need to increase our ranks."

Master Parry, who was very astute and always in the thick of everything Protestant, smiled a knowing smile at me as he asked, "of what sort of people would my lady be wanting?"

I looked at them both in turn. "Men, I should think. Men who can handle… a weapon." I said the last quietly. I hoped that they would sense my meaning and know that it was possible that we might have to fight for our freedom soon.

Not two weeks later, I had a visit from a Scottish man I had never met in my life: Sir James Croft. He called at Ashridge, however I was out with my horse and did not receive him. Sir John did and said he stayed for over half an hour waiting for me. I was glad to miss him though, for I knew him to be in collaboration with the rebellion and I hoped desperately that none of Mary's spies had seen him.

I was suspicious though, for within a few days, I received a letter from Mary insisting that I join her at Whitehall. "There is a rebellion in the countryside. I am still angry with you, but I would not want harm to befall you. I would have you join me at court for your own safety. Be assured that you may stay as long as you like and that I, in this dire time, will welcome you heartily." Her postscripts ensured me that, regardless of rumors floating about and of what efforts I had made to secure my own safety, she would never condemn a dear sister without answer and due proof.

This did little to reassure me. I understood what this letter said, and I began to fear for my life. Mary was attempting to lure me to London. I would not go, but how best to ignore an express command from the queen? After much consideration, I wrote her back.

Your Majesty,

Thank you so much for your kind letter. I wish to apologize for my ignorance and for my impertinence last time we met.

I was so happy to receive your letter, however, alas, you have found me in my sick bed. I fear that my horrid state began when you sent me away. I was so overwhelmed with grief at my misstep that I have made myself unable to travel. My head and stomach pain me so that I can barely move.

Please know that I would do all that you ask, only have mercy on me. As soon as I am recovered, I will meet with you at Whitehall.

Furthermore, I do not believe that the rebels will get as far as Hertfordshire, they will probably not even leave their homes. I do not think you have anything to fear, my sister, for God is on your side.

With love,
Elizabeth

February 1554
Ashridge House, Hertfordshire

I received two bits of horrible news at once. First, Mary had signed Robert's death warrant. The moment this news filled my ears, my heart dropped out of my feet. I wanted to rush to him. For the first time since Kett's rebellion, I considered fully what Robert's death would do to me. It was too awful to dwell on. I found myself truly sick with the prospect. Mary was vindictive for certain. She was angry with me, and I was disobeying her. She knew she had Robert and that I cared for him. She was trying to force my obedience.

The news of four thousand men marching on London with Sir Thomas Wyatt at the head gave me a sliver of hope that I could come up with a way to save Robert, for Mary, with any luck, would be too busy to worry about executing him for the time being.

Chancellor Gardiner had proven himself and found the plot out, thus Mary was prepared. She rallied London with lies that a marriage treaty with Spain was out of the question. She told them of her love and loyalty and promised all her devotion, for she was one of them... their prince. With that she had all of London at her disposal and, despite the rebels' impressive force, she handled them as a babe its clouts.

Only two days after Mary had arrested the rebels, I sat in my sitting room at Hatfield waiting for the soldiers to arrive. Edward Courtenay had been involved in the rebellion and, when brought to the question, had insinuated that I was to be queen and him king when the whole mess was done. That was his ploy. I hadn't figured it out, though I knew something was amiss with his out-of-the-blue proposal.

However, this was not all. Mary's minions had collected several pieces of information that seemed to denounce me as a traitor.

Despite all my forethought, I could not help but be implicated in a plot to take down the queen, for who had more motivation than me?

Kat and John sat with me and looked nervously one to another as we waited. Finally, I broke the silence. "You know I had no part in this, do you not?"

They spoke on top of one another. "Of course not," said John.

"We would never think such a thing," Kat insisted.

After a while, Kat cleared her throat and said, "I am afraid of returning to the Tower, my lady." A single tear leaked from her eye and Sir John held her hand tightly.

"None of us will be sent to the Tower if they will just let me talk to Mary. I know that I can convince her of my innocence."

"I wonder why she has not written you back."

I wondered the same thing. "I fear I must buy us some time. I know that if I can somehow get Mary a letter, she will agree to see me." I looked at Kat and said, "I must take to my bed and see if I cannot wait Mary out."

"I agree with you. I will arrange everything. Quickly go to your chambers, my lady. For I fear the soldiers are upon us."

Several hours later, a half a dozen soldiers accompanied two of Mary's councilors, the Earl of Sussex and the Marquess of Winchester. Before they even talked with me, they summoned a doctor. Sir John told them of my sickness and that I was unable to leave my bed or receive anyone. The doctor came and when he entered my room, Sussex and Winchester decided they were welcome, too.

Instantly, I surrounded myself with the power prepared to do as I must, but the doctor surprised me as he sat, slicing me deeply with a small knife he kept up his sleeve. I cried out in pain… and lost my light.

It was clear they had conspired against me. This one thing was enough to send the men out of the room, convinced that I was feigning illness. Afterward, the doctor did exam me, but why should it matter what his findings were? The men had seen what they needed.

The doctor concluded that I was well enough for travel, and that was how I found myself in a litter on my way to London. I allowed this to happen, for I knew that if I could only get before Mary, all would be made right.

Each day was horrid. I forced the company to go as slowly as possible, all the while hoping to meet a courier on the way with a letter of response from Mary. I could but manipulate the lot of them, but I had learned better. That would only serve as a temporary solution, and one that might cost these men their lives.

Soon, I truly began to feel sick. I worried at every second, so much so that my stomach was in knots and I could not eat at all. All of my follies haunted me. Mary had every cause to execute me; I had not stood up to the rebels as I should have. I had been a bad sister and subject.

I was in deep despair knowing that I would never see Robert again. Or Kat, to whom I cried, "Mary is going to kill me, and I will never see those I love again."

"No, my lady, no. She will not do so, for you are innocent. She has no desire to have innocent blood on her hands."

"I do not know what she wants. All I know is that I feel it. She will kill me. My only hope is that she will let me die with dignity, like my mother did."

"Do not say it, my lady." She cradled my hand to her breast. "Shush now. Try and get some rest."

I overheard some of the men talking that afternoon, and it began a boiling in my blood that finally lent my spine some strength.

"Renard said that she is pregnant with a sailor's child."

"No, I heard it was a stableman."

"I suppose I am glad of it. I feel we need to have a reason to treat a Tudor this way. It feels wrong."

"Pregnant or not, Tudor or not, she could not make this journey go any slower if she had leprosy."

I pulled back the curtain of my litter and looked over at the men. "You will not speak thus! For I am a princess..."

Both Sussex and Winchester were riding not far from my litter, but their faces held horror as they looked at me.

"Pardon, my lady, but your face."

"You are all swollen up."

"And covered with lumps."

"Quick man, fetch the doctor." Sussex said to a soldier.

Quick-witted John thought to chide the men, "You see, you sons of goats, we said she was sick. If she perishes on your watch, may God have mercy on your souls."

I could have kissed him.

We stopped for several days while I rested in earnest. I was swollen all over and the lumps that plagued me disfigured my face. The doctor had no name for my sickness, but I heard them whispering about guilt and God's retribution.

There was nothing to do. Kat stayed at my side, and, before long, the swellings were abating, and we were again heading toward London and death.

I dressed in white the day we entered London. The crowds around us cheered and yelled their allegiance and love... not to Mary, but to me. I wanted to silence them, for they would only make things worse. I had pulled back the curtains of my litter, though, and as I saw the soldiers surrounding me for protection, my focus could not entirely ignore the Tower that stood dauntingly before us.

I wondered if Robert was looking out one of those windows. Could he see us all? Me? I hoped he could, for it might be the last time.

We did not continue on toward the Tower, but turned west toward Whitehall.

Once at Whitehall, I immediately petitioned to see Mary, but she would not see me or receive any letters from me. I overheard some maids gossiping about how the queen was out for blood. They were the ones who informed me that Mary had killed poor Jane and Guildford. They had been beheaded. She was killing off all her rivals for the throne. This news sent me almost into hysterics. If not for the friendly faces of Kat and Blanche, I would have fainted from fear and never rose again.

I lay in bed and waited with my faithful ladies at my side, panic gripping me at every moment. Two days later, I learned that they had William St. Loe, my messenger, in hand and were questioning him.

"Heaven help me! If they were able to get their hands on Sir William, is it possible that they can get ahold of the most damning bit of evidence there could be?" I said quietly to myself and threw the blankets over my head. I had tossed Wyatt's letter into the fire immediately upon reading it, but it seemed it did not matter. They could probably resurrect it somehow. After all, Mary was quite saintly.

I feared they somehow knew of the letter, or soon would, for they also had Wyatt and were torturing him for information as I lay there. I knew that I must tell them first thing about the letter, but how?

March 1554
Whitehall Palace, London

Weeks passed in the same fashion. I spent the entire time under guard and unable to have any visitors. Finally, on the
seventeenth of March, the entire council summoned me to
inform me of my charges.

"You have been charged with treason against her majesty the queen
and illegal communication with the enemy France." Gardiner said with a
vicious smile.

I was still in shock. Mary had invited me to stay with her, and now
I was being charged and those charges so ridiculous. I was astounded.
"But sirs, I have done nothing against her majesty, my sister!" I protest-
ed.

"That will be discovered in your trial. For now, it is known that you
were involved in the Wyatt conspiracies and that, in and of itself, will
cost you dearly."

I again protested, "I have done nothing of the sort! I have never met
the man. I…"

"Save your lies for the trial. Make yourself ready. You are to be
taken to the Tower, by order of the queen. However, we will not do so
now, for it's after dark and we would fear escaped rebels may rescue you
as we float the river." With those comments, he left me stunned.

There were upwards of twenty men in the room and once my protests had ended, I pulled the light to me and formed two dozen balls of light which I flung around the room in a desperate manner. "You will all see that I am innocent. You will tell the queen."

I watched as the incredible power my mother and grandmothers had gifted me worked its way into the minds of these men. I saw their countenances change, and as the guards pulled me out of the chamber and toward my room, I hoped I had taken advantage of all the opportunities I could to proclaim myself innocent.

In my room, my mind went over and over this dreadful debacle. I was to go to the Tower, and Robert was there. Perhaps... perhaps, I could save us both.

That night, I dreamed of Robert's face as he watched me lie on the headsman's block, and I hoped and prayed with all my heart that it was not one of my discernments.

I awoke early that morning with such a headache that the light hurt my eyes. Before I could rub the sleep out of them, Sussex and Winchester were at my door demanding it was time to go. After a night of terrifying dreams, I felt this was my end if I did not do something more to save myself. I cried and pleaded with them to let me write to Mary. I pleaded and cajoled and when they would not permit me, I took it to the next level. Filling myself with the power, I convinced them that I would write a letter and they would wait until I was finished. I could not care what Mary would do to them. I was too frightened for my own life.

Sussex was instantly convinced, but my manipulation had next to no effect on Winchester. Of course, I had been very careful, but it was interesting to see which mind was stronger, or perhaps, which man was more sympathetic to my plight.

I began knowing that I would draw this process out as long as I could, for the next day was Palm Sunday, a Holy day, and I hoped that they would not take me to the Tower on that holiday. I only hoped though.

My *beloved Queen and sister,*

I have much to say to you concerning this predicament. I beg of you to see me, for I know many a life would be saved if the princess of our land would only talk to their prisoners before condemning them. For how could you denounce a relative without talking to them directly? You yourself promised me with the love of a sister that you would not condemn me without answer or due proof. I beg of you, fulfill that promise to me by seeing me before you send me to the Tower.

 I must tell you just in case you will not see me, that I am innocent. The traitor Wyatt can write letters to anyone he pleases and whether I received one from him or not is immaterial. What matters is this: have I done anything against you? The answer: I have never stepped against you in any way.

 As for a letter sent to the French king, I pray that God will confound me eternally if I ever sent him a word, message, token, or letter. I give you my word that I have not participated, planned, talked of, or even thought of rebellion. I have not asked anyone to implement any particular of Wyatt's plan, nor have I any knowledge of the plan's particulars.

 I have done nothing wrong. I promise this to you, and is not the promise of a princess worth more than that of other men?

 I know that men speak in your ear and tell you that you will not be safe with me alive, but I tell you that I have proven to you that I am on your side, that you benefit from the information I can collect. You know what circumstances I speak of. I pray that you will not let these evil manipulators persuade you against me, your only sister.

 Furthermore, must I always be among the plotters because we have the same father? Must I always be vying for the throne just because one day it could be mine? No! You never did so with Edward. I have not, nor will I ever do so with you. These are the ideas of men with a guilty disposition. They are who would do such things, not I, the humble servant of your majesty.

I pray to God that you will hear my cry and answer my plea, for I feel that I should not be condemned before the sight of men before the whole truth is known. I humbly crave but one word of answer from you.

Your highness' most faithful subject, that has been from the beginning and will be to my end.

Elizabeth

I read it over and over, correcting things and adding words that I had left out in my haste. In the end, I feared that words could be added to the letter by my enemies, for I had only written but a few lines on the second page, so I hastily crossed out the empty space, then added my signature to the bottom.

Once I was satisfied, I gingerly handed the letter to Sussex as Winchester stated, "you took your time, my lady. The tide has returned, and it will not go until midnight and you know very well that we cannot go then. I suppose it will be on the Sabbath that you shall be taken to the Tower."

"Is tomorrow not Palm Sunday, my Lords?" I asked.

"Yes, it is, and a good thing too; many more people will be in church and not on the banks of the river to see you." Sussex said obligingly.

He did not know that I wanted the people to see me. I hoped that they would speak out in my behalf… that they would let Mary know that what she was doing was not acceptable. She should not flippantly send a princess to the Tower. Not without a chance for said princess to prove herself first.

Regardless, I watched as the men left and knew that Mary would read the letter whether she liked it or not. For Sussex had disregarded her orders and allowed me to write it.

Also, I was glad to have delayed going to the Tower, for me, and for Kat, for though I was now separated from her, she would be going with me to that dreaded place.

The morning was cold and the water colder. Some had seeped in as we hit river bottom while going under London Bridge. I pulled the light to me and asked the water to exit my shoes, which it did. I had not used this talent in a while and honestly, I forgot I had it. Manipulation and discernment were my main sources of power, but I wondered if there was a way the water could help me. I set my mind to the task of pondering that puzzle so that fear would not get the better of me.

Before it seemed possible, we landed at Tower Wharf. Winchester, Sussex, and Sir John Gage exited the boat before me, and Sussex was kind enough to help me out. He looked drained and I felt terrible that my fear had cost him. I was sure that Mary had given him the tongue lashing of a lifetime for taking my letter. Alas, it did no good, for she did not even send me a word of reply, only guards to take me to the Tower.

I looked up to the Tower as I walked across the drawbridge, and my thoughts flitted to Robert for a moment. This was the closest I had been to him in a year.

My thoughts were taken from him as a momentous animalistic roar filled the narrow causeway we passed. I was so startled that I instantly pulled Sussex to me. He looked at me with pity and I let him go instantly with an apology. They were marching me past the menagerie. Was this to frighten me? As if I needed to be more frightened.

Next, I was to be marched past every guard in the Tower, it seemed. "These men cannot be here for me, for I am only one woman," I said uncomfortably. Why was Mary showing me her might in such a way? Did she think I would speak and call down an army from heaven?

"No, madam," Sir John replied, "it is only custom."

I soon saw more to give me alarm, for I was walked right by the scaffolding where Jane, Guildford, and my mother had most likely been executed.

At this moment, my small courage vanished, and tears began to drip down my face. One of the guards saw me crying and went to his knee, saying, "God save your grace!"

I was moved as several other men removed their caps and some also knelt. The people did love me after all, even these armed men. Perhaps my cause was not so hopeless at that.

Finally, we reached the royal palace at the center of the Tower. Sussex leaned into me and whispered, "these apartments were redone by your father for your mother."

I looked up to him with surprise. "In truth?" I asked.

"Yes, my lady."

I smiled as Winchester took out a grand key and unlocked the door. He kept the key out and that told me that he would be locking me in. Sussex held the door open for me and I walked into the beautifully furnished apartment.

But before he closed the door, I heard Sussex talk sternly to Winchester and Gage. "What will you do, my lords? She is a king's daughter and the queen's sister." I watched the door shut and heard the key lock it. However, I also heard Sussex, though the door, continue his protest. "You have not been commissioned to do so; she should not be locked in like she was in a cell. I fear if you do more than commanded, you will answer for it hereafter."

They walked away and so I heard no more. Sussex was a good and true fellow. I would remember him.

I woke with a start. It was still dark. Sleep had not come easy since I arrived at the Tower, and when it did come, it was filled with startling dreams. I reviewed the dream that had just passed through my mind with unusual clarity.

My mother was here in these apartments, and she was scraping and prying at a stone in the hearth. I saw her so clearly, it was amazing. It was if I watched her in front of me. Her black hair and dark looks, I had never seen before, that I remembered. She was gloriously beautiful. No wonder father was taken so fully with her.

Finally, she got the stone loose and I watched as she took a letter, tied with a white ribbon, and laid it in the space. Then she laid the stone back on top of the page. I saw her look to the side and smile to herself. It was a secretive smile that made me very curious.

I also saw in my dream Robert dead. Beautiful eyes glazed over, brown curls askance. Blood. I knew, knew that Robert was going to die. I felt it in my bones. I feared that I was going to die. I had to do something. I had so much to tell Robert. I had forgiveness to offer him. I had promises to renew. I had kisses to give him. I could not die without expressing my undying love to him. For all I knew, Robert was no more than twenty steps away from me.

I stood and paced in the light of the moon. What could I do? This was a cell. All doors locked, all windows barred... but, perhaps, I could open the window.

Following the light of the moon, I went to the window and unlatched it. Pushing it open, I instinctually pulled the light to me. Uncertain why, only just letting myself be led by a power greater than myself.

Walking on the cobbled path below me was my guard. The man brought me food and took my chamber pot. He had my key, and more than that, was one of those who had knelt before me when I arrived. I wondered how I could use him to help me see Robert.

The answer came quickly, and I obeyed the idea. I sent an urgent thought to him that he needed to check on me. As the light hit him, he looked up to my window and began rushing up the steps.

I paced. I hadn't thought of something like this before. Escape was against my nature, but was that what I was doing? No. I could not. That would secure the death of Kat and Robert and Master Parry and John. I had to see this through. For Mary would not hesitate to punish my favorites in my stead.

I would go to Robert. Hold him. Tell him my secrets. Tell him I loved him. And I would come back and face my sister. Yes.

I heard the key in the door.

And rung my hands nervously, asking that other sense what to do next. The moment the door opened, I knew what to do. I told the man with my power to strip his clothes off and hand over the keys. I asked him where Robert was, and I was not surprised to find that he was in the small rooms on the bottom floor of my same Tower. My officer had the keys to this Tower and thus I had what I needed. I put a dark cloth over my hair and told the man in his small clothes to wait in my room for me and to not think or talk. I sent the largest ball of light to him and he instantly went listless and still.

Knowing he would stay until I came back, I took a deep breath and stole out of my room. I moved as quietly as I could down the stairs and down the hall to the room I'd learned was Robert's. Pulling out the keys, I tried them until I found the one that fit.

As I entered, I saw Robert was sitting up, the moon light from his window shining right on his bed. I could see him rather well and as I examine his rather dirty, bearded face, I felt everything that made me who I am gather, coalesce, and settle into rightness.

"Robert," I whispered.

He paused, rising from his bed, his head whipping toward me. Then he was rushing at me. "Elizabeth?"

"Yes," I whispered.

And he was in my arms. "Oh, my darling. How…" He pulled the cloth off my hair and took my face in his hands. "How are you here?" His voice, his breath, his face. Him.

Tears began running as I said, "does it really matter?" And our eyes found each other's. I saw all I needed to there. He loved me. He loved me.

There was no decision made. There was no thinking. There was just life and death and us.

We went for each other in the same moment. Our lips colliding in a frenzied passion I could not keep up with. I only knew that I felt everything. Every touch, every breath, his mouth, his tongue, his hands. I basked and reveled and wanted more.

When Robert bent and took me under my thighs and lifted me, my legs naturally wrapped around him because of the freedom of the pants I wore. It surprised me and delighted me. It felt powerful. I squeezed him with my legs and pressed my mouth harder into his, taking his hair in my hands, so his head and body were submitted to me.

He did not seem to mind, for his hands were busy exploring the parts of me he loved.

It did not take long before I could no longer manage the desires inside me, they were too big, too overwhelming. I wanted him. Every last inch of him.

I let my legs loose and because Robert had such a good hold on my buttocks, I slid down him in a manner that promised everything. We separated enough to look into one another's eyes.

"I love you. I am so sorry we have been separated. I am so sorry I pushed you away," I said, and I took hold of his shirt tail, pulling it over his head and discarding it. I flattened my palms against his flat stomach and smoothed them up his taut chest, circling the small patch of hair between his pectoral muscles. My lust deepened as I admired his body. When my eyes made it back up to his, I demanded, "I will have you now, like this is the last night of my life."

He took my face in his hands and searched my eyes, uncertain. When he found only love and iron will and unadulterated desire, he kissed me so completely, so tenderly I couldn't help but cry for so many wasted years and lost hopes and bygone chances.

I hovered over Robert, sweaty and exuberate and almost finished. The moon shimmered through the window and it almost felt like she smiled down on us as we moved together. She knew what would happen if I let him spend himself inside of me.

I had not chosen yet. I knew I did not want to be a mother. But the chances of that were low, besides I could be dead tomorrow. What would a fillos child, conceived by moonlight, matter if the mother was dead? So, I did not stop him. Instead, I reveled in it and gave as much as I received.

But I had to tell him. I had to.

I would. Later.

"Robert."

"My love."

"We need to talk about something."

The man beside me in the moonlight pushed dark curls out of his eyes and rose up on his elbow, his eyes intent upon me.

I cleared my throat. "Well, I made you a promise and I need to keep it, just in case…"

He shook his head, stubbornly. "No, no! This will not be a goodbye speech. I will not listen." He turned and flopped back onto his back.

I sat up in bed and moved my hair out of the way and pulled a blanket across my chest. "I want to tell you of my gift." I felt him go stiff. So, I turned and looked at him. I waited. Then I surrounded myself with the power, filling the room with light.

At this Robert slowly sat up, his eyes only on me. He reached for me. Touching my luminous skin, he said, "Beautiful." Fingertips as gentle as a feather, he traced the curve of my jaw to my throat where he wrapped his large hand around the back of my neck and pulled me to him. His eyes watched me as I came close and when our lips met, he seemed tentative.

I felt something interesting while so close and in the thrall of my power. Once Robert came with in my light, I could feel him, not with my hands, but with my mind. I could sense his awe, and desire, and fear. It made his kiss so much more impactful and I felt overwhelmed by him.

I allowed Robert to do what he wanted, for I imagined he'd wanted this for a long while, so transfixed was he when he saw my light. He kissed and caressed my glowing skin, staring into my eyes and looking with awe.

I enjoyed watching him and touching him also. He was so beautiful and good.

Finally, I saw the light in the sky change from moonlight to astronomical dawn and I knew that I had to talk to him. "Robert my love. I must leave soon. Can we talk?"

Robert sighed and flopped back down on his back. "I think my life has reached its apex. Here in the dank prison cell, all because of you. It is as if I just made love to an angel. I have no words."

"I feel like that might be a bit sacrilegious, don't you? What we just did is called adultery, Robert, and we probably will burn in hell for the rest of our existence because Mary is going to kill us any day now and we will not have time to do enough Hail Mary's to make it right."

Robert laughed out loud for a full minute. I did too, because I didn't believe in the Hail Mary. I was Protestant.

When he calmed down a bit, he shook his head at me; "We will not burn, my love, for we are married."

I squinted at him. "Yes, in our hearts. But you, my love, have a wife that is not me."

He shook his head at me. "You do not understand. I am married to you and only you. I have not consummated with Amy, ever. Any forced marital union with Amy has never existed, not in the law nor in my heart. I have made it so. I thought you understood this. Only you exist."

Once again, this man surprised me and crushed me in the same moment. "How? How Robert?"

He pushed my hair back. "Do you have any idea who you are? What you do to me? How could I be tempted by Amy?" He almost said it with disgust. "Elizabeth, I did not make that promise to you, so many years ago in your room at Hatfield, frivolously."

"But...two years we've been apart."

"That was how long you needed. I, and my father, have asked a terrible thing of you. A terrible, lonely, dangerous life. The least I could do in return is vow fidelity and so I did. You were there, my love. You have my fidelity and so much more of me. You always have."

Shocked, I answered, "I do not understand you, Robert Dudley. But I promise I will never doubt you again." I began to cry. Slowly at first and then nastily. He pulled me to him and stroked my hair.

After I calmed down, we sat in silence, our minds working on separate thoughts. Until I spoke. "I am sorry about your father and your brother, Robert."

He took a moment to answer. "Thank you, as am I."

"Who knows, we may join them soon enough."

"Yes, and if I see my father again, I might just kill him a second time."

I looked at him. "He was not really a good man, but Robert, are you not sad that he is gone?"

"I am sad, sad that he died in his folly. I do wish him peace, though."

I leaned back against him and nodded slightly and felt exactly how I felt regarding my father. We held each other until the sun rose, not knowing if this was the last time we would be able to do so.

I played the same trick with my guard the next night. Robert sat on the bed waiting for me. Hope in his eyes and joy when he saw me.

I breathed between kisses and said, "Robert, if you do not take me now, I might die, but I did not come for this. There is something very important about my gift I must tell you."

His hands and mouth were busy, but he lifted his head to say, "whatever it is, I accepted you and your gift long ago. I will do anything I can to protect you."

"Even raise a child by yourself?" I closed my eyes, reveling in his touch, only half my mind on our conversation.

"A child?" He slowed and I looked down at him.

"It is what I have been wanting to tell you about my gift." Robert completely stopped, and I growled at him, "Do not even think about stopping."

"As you wish, but I am anxious to have this conversation."

"Stop talking, sir."

He nodded and I lost myself in the man I knew I could never be parted from again, the man I loved with every inch of my soul. The man who was my husband.

"What time do they bring your food?"

"Not until tenth bell."

"I'm sure I will get mine sooner than that." I had on my shift and was putting the guard's uniform on just to be ready.

"I am feeling a bit eager to hear your tale, my love."

I nodded after the shirt was over my head. "I will tell you the basics. My gift gives me certain abilities."

"Yes, like making people do what you want."

I smiled at him. "Yes, I can manipulate people's minds. Make them do basically anything I want them to do, and I can tell them to believe something that they would not normally believe, and I can confuse them so much that they will not see what I do not want them to see."

Any other time I had wanted to tell Robert my secret, the words would not come, but suddenly, somehow, the opposite happened. Perhaps it was the new and unexpectedly deep commitment I felt toward him. It was as if we had been through enough hardship, trial, and testing that we suddenly knew the spider-silk fine commitment we had made so long ago was not weak at all, it was like iron. And we had possibly made a baby together.

Words poured out in completely coherent sentences. "I can convince them that hopping on one foot from London to the border of Scotland would be a wonderful waste of a month and they would do it. I can make them love me or hate their loved ones; though I have found that messing with strong emotions is very dangerous. It is what my mother did, and you see where it got her." Robert's mouth dropped open like a codfish, but I did not let him speak. "Yes, my mother was the same as me and so was my grandmothers as far back as forever. So, I can also manipulate water as you well remember, I am sure. I can make it do what I want, though I am only beginning to learn about this aspect. Lastly, I can see the future in my dreams... at times... and only brief glimpses. My grandmother said that her gift of foretelling did not really mature until she was above twenty." Again, with Robert and his shocked mouth and again, I did not let him speak. "I am the most talented of all my ancestors that I have read about. Consequently, I have developed a rather strict set of rules that I force myself to abide by... most of the time. Of course, those rules have been developed by my mistakes. Every daughter who does not have someone to guide her must learn and struggle on her own. I was lucky, though; my mother and grandmother went to great effort to see that I was able to get enough information so that I could at least know what was happening to me."

I paused and knowing finally lit Robert's eyes. "That letter from your mother...the one you and Kat received at Hatfield just after I met you, was that about this?"

"That is when I learned I was a daughter of the moon and mind, or a Fillos."

"Daughter of the moon and the mind, huh? It's a good thing that I have had plenty of time to get used to the idea that you had some kind of... something." He looked down at me seriously. "I will admit that I have always been a believer in the mystical, but this does not seem like that. You are so filled with light when you have the power in you... it cannot be something evil, it cannot." He laughed tightly. "And I suppose if I cast all reason aside, it does not sound so horrific. Strange? Yes. Otherworldly? Yes. But, beautiful too." He touched my cheek.

I bit my lip, "A power you would trust enough to have passed down to a daughter?"

He looked over at me again, confused.

I took in a deep breath and I could see Robert's body stiffen, but I plunged on. "There is but one way, that I know of, for this gift to be passed on; and be passed on, it must."

I waited, and he waited as we looked into one another's eyes and, to my surprise, after several long moments, Robert said, "I see the fear in your eyes and I know what that fear means. You must pass it on by giving birth to one with the gift, mustn't you?" His eyes held uncertainty. "And I just helped you to do so, didn't I?" Then they held anger.

"I wanted to tell you before, so it would be a choice. Please do not be angry. I did not plan on any of this, I just had to see you again, in case..."

"In case we die tomorrow," Robert said a bit petulantly.

He needed time to process, and I needed to go back and relieve my guard so that he would not get into trouble. The sun was rising high into the morning sky. "You need to think. Please believe me that I came only to see you. After the last two years, how could I know it would go this way? I did not plan this out. But once we were in the mist of it, I did not stop it. I was like a regular wife. Allowing what is natural to take place. It was a moment's decision. Still, I love you."

He went to the door and opened it.

I moved to him. "Please forgive me. Please live. Please. I will be doing everything I can to get to Mary and if I can get to Mary, I can force her to change her mind." I kissed him. "Thank you. Thank you so much for being the man that you are. Thank you for trusting and loving me for so many years... even when you got nothing in return. This secret of mine could have ruined us, you know." I swallowed hard and my voice intensified. "Yet, because of you, it has only pulled us together. Your patience and trust, and your acceptance, have changed my entire existence," I whispered to him, then I touched his face again. "Robert." Tears instantly sprang to my eyes. "You are everything to me. I would face my fears for you. I would risk my life for you. I would have a child for you, just so that more of you would be in the world. You bring me joy. My cup runneth over, my love." I took him in my arms and kissed him and then I left, locking his door behind me.

I arrived back at my room to a stone-still guard, waiting patiently as I told him to. He looked very cold. I stoked the fire and led him to it. I pulled my light to me and told him to put the clothes on I had just thrown off. No sooner was his last buckle fastened, than my door burst open to two guards.

"There you are, Lieutenant Blanchard, where have you been? You missed roll call!"

I rose from my chair, throwing a ball of power toward Blanchard, releasing him from my grasp, and readied a ball of light for all three men just in case this went badly.

But Blanchard took care of it himself; he shook his head and looked around. "I have no idea what I am doing here." He looked at me and pointed. "I came to check on her and then I remember nothing. I must have blacked out again."

I blinked at him. How perfect this was.

The guards turned to me. "What do you know of this, my lady?"

"Sirs, did not we just wake with the sunrise? How am I to know what men of action do while the rest of us sleep?"

It was that easy.

"You are going to get the lash if Arnold has his way," the older of the two guards said, and pulled Bridges to the door.

Closing it, they locked it behind them. I sighed in relief, sinking back into a chair exhausted and, within moments, fell asleep.

Over the next four nights, I did not have another opportunity to see Robert. I only hoped I had done enough.

I had dreamt that dream about my mother several times every night. However, tonight it was so clear, so crisp, it was as if I were in the same room as my mother, watching her do her job.

Tomorrow I was to go on trial and with how quickly Mary took care of the Dudleys, I feared that this could be my last night on the earth. Thus, I got out of bed and went to the fireplace in the sitting room. Instantly I saw the stone that I knew would be loose. Taking the shovel, I pushed the coals to one side and blew the ash away before taking the poker and working at the stone. At length, it moved, and soon, I had it out. Carefully, I reached my hand in the crevasse and, to my amazement, pulled out the letter with the ribbon.

My hands shook as I turned it over and saw my name written on the outside in a hand I knew. I closed my eyes and took a deep breath. How could I be so fortunate as to have another letter from my mother? I wondered how many little things had to happen in order for me to receive this into my hands.

God was great and wonderful.

I slipped the ribbon off and unfolded the pages. At the top was the date. 18 May 1536. This letter was written the day before she was killed. I bowed my head over the letter. A few tears ran down my cheeks as I thought of my mother awaiting her death in this very room; and as one of her last acts, she wrote a letter to me.

My darling Elizabeth,

God has given me a great gift; though I no longer have my gifts, he still has shown you to me. I cannot tell you how beautiful you are. In my dreams this night I watched you take a letter out of the hearth of this very room in the Tower. I knew that it was a letter from me and so I am here, writing a letter, so you have something to find. I cannot think of what else to say, yet I have so many things I wish to tell you. I love you. I am proud of all you are.

God has shown me the woman that you will become. Though I cannot tell you all, I will tell you this: you will fulfill my dreams and wishes for you, and do things I never imagined possible. This one statement should tell you enough about your current predicament to bring you comfort, for you should be comforted. None can take your life, not even Mary, for you are destined for great things and God is the one who made the plan. Do what you must to pacify Mary, for she is capable of much evil. But God will not be thwarted in his plans, even if all the princes of the world be at your door threatening you. Know this, my daughter, and be at peace.

I love you and wish that I could be near you. You are truly the most powerful fillos of us all. Thank the Lord for your great-grandmother's scheme. She was the one who thought to make one extremely powerful daughter by relinquishing gifts from mother to daughter. I admit, we all hoped it would be me who ruled; however, God has a different path for me.

I can congratulate myself for all I have accomplished, but now it is time for me to pay the consequence. Henry will take my life very soon, but I do not fear, my daughter, for I know that I did what God gave me power to do. All will be right, and generations from now, the powerful men of this earth will be amazed at the reformation that we started. Of course, they will never give us credit, but it matters not, for we know the truth and God knows the truth.

I hope that you will find a way to reserve your power for that which God calls you to do, and not take advantage of all around you. You have been born with a gift that requires a higher standard of consciousness. Please make every effort to strengthen yourself against the evil one.

Live well, my daughter, and find something that is yours and hold to it.

Do not let yourself be so caught up in your responsibilities that you neglect to find joy in this amazing experience God has given you. Life is the most intriguing journey there is, because it is the only journey. Please excuse all the trite advice, I say all this wanting to have my part of making you the woman you become. Oh, that I could watch and see all you shall accomplish!

> *God bless you and keep you.*
> *With all the love In my heart.*
> *Your mother Anne Boleyn*

How amazing to have this precious scrap of paper. How I thanked Mary for putting me in the Tower so that I could acquire it. I felt joy at my mother's sentiments, relief at her revelations, and strength from her faith. I pressed the letter to my heart and walked slowly back to my bed. There, I thought of all she told me until the moonlight crept through the drapes.

I faced the council with confidence and conviction. They would not get the better of me. Lord George Cornwallis presently stood and faced me civilly. "Madam, you are here to answer for your involvement in the Wyatt Rebellion. The charges are thus: that you knew of and supported the rebellion."

"I know the charges, my lords, and I stand before you full of righteous indignation, for I am completely innocent of any and all crimes that I am accused." My voice was steady, my attitude superior. I was sure my mother and father would be proud of me.

"What were you to do at Donnington?" Cornwallis asked, ignoring my speech, though many in the room looked uncomfortably about. I instantly discerned that these men where the ones on my side. It was good to know that I did have some friends in the crowd.

"More materially, why would you talk of moving yourself to Donnington if you did not know of the rebellion?" Bishop Gardiner asked in his deep voice and glared at Cornwallis.

"Gentlemen, please, relieve my mind at once, what is all this talk of

Donnington? I know neither about Donnington nor where it is."

Winchester laughed, "Are we expected to believe she is not even aware of a castle that is hers by acquisition? This must be a farce."

"I have many houses, my lord," I said as sharply as I could to Winchester. "If I own this castle, I have never slept there."

Gardiner sighed heavily and said, "bring in Sir James."

I waited as the soldiers brought the man in and when I saw him, I finally remembered myself. Instantly, I spoke up. "Yes, this man did pay me a visit. I had forgotten him until I saw his face. He also, as I remember, was attempting to get Master Parry to move me from Ashridge to some other place... Donnington, I assume?" I paused thoughtfully. "As I recall, he was worried over my safety, a bit strange for a man I did not know as even an acquaintance. Though... many are worried for me as I know you have seen proof." Looking away from the man's face, I turned back to the council. "I am assuming that he is a rebel. Well, send him out, I have no desire to be in the same room with anyone thus connected." To my surprise, Gardiner nodded, and they took him out. "Where, may I ask, does this questioning go? I have the right to be visited and I have the right to go to any or all of my houses whenever I please, do I not?"

It was then that the Earl of Arundel stood. "This is folly, my lords. She has not involved herself with this plot! She is to be our next queen, I remind you all, and I, for one, will not be a party to troubling her in so vain a matter." He turned to me and bowed as he said, "I hope that you would forgive me, your highness." Shocked, I only nodded deferentially to him and with that, he sat and turned himself away from the crowd.

Gardiner looked to me and scowled. "Do not be so haughty, my lady, for there is mounting evidence against you. You will be singing a different tune once we wring Wyatt dry of information. He has already admitted to writing to you. He said your response was not at all unfavorable."

I was utterly shocked. "How dare you speak to me thus. There can be no evidence unless it is of your contrivance. We have had this conversation. Once again, let me be clear, I am innocent. I was not involved in the plot in the slightest way, and may God strike me down, Bishop, if I am telling a falsehood."

Bishop Gardiner rose suddenly and turned about, muttering aloud, "there is nothing more to be done today, my Lords." And he left the room.

Kat and Blanche sat in my room when I came back from questioning. Kat jumped to her feet at seeing me and said kindly, after embracing me, "My lady, you do look so pale and thin, are they feeding you properly?"

"Yes, Kat, they have been surprisingly kind. Sir John Bridges is vehemently against my stay here, though he supports Mary as he would a goddess, and thus sees to my comfort. I just returned from being questioned and I must say, I got the upper hand. Also, the guards and many of the council see that I am innocent and fear me as their next queen."

"Yet, you do have enemies here."

"Yes, of course I do. Many consider me a traitor," I said sadly.

"It is only… while I was out, I heard that there was a plot to poison you."

"Heaven forbid!" Blanche shouted.

"That would be a truly dreadful way to meet my end," I answered seriously, but with a twinkle in my eye.

"Do not jest, my lady! I have never been more scared for you in my life," Kat said, her voice trembling a bit.

"I have most certainly been more frightened for myself, Kat. Think of when Lady Tyrwhitt lived with us. Now that was a slow death like none I would wish on my enemy."

"Elizabeth, be serious."

I smiled. "I am sorry, Kat. I just cannot help but think I am going to make it through alright. At least, I have not been poisoned yet. I do not think it impossible, though."

"We must watch and be wary," she said, eyes large and serious.

"Yes, we must indeed." Still, I knew that it would not happen, for my mother had seen me alive and well and old. The comfort that letter brought me was astounding and I thanked God over and over again for leading her to write it.

For the moment, with the stress of the questioning behind me and the letter from my mother buoying me up, my mind wandered to Robert. His beautiful face filled my mind and I wondered how he fared. What he would say to me if I saw him again. Would he be angry? I dreamed of seeing him again. Of being with him. I had felt no change in myself as far as a child might be concerned and, in part, felt relief that we were not successful. Still I worried dreadfully over him. Mary had condemned him to death, and though she had stayed her hand because of my manipulation, that did not guarantee all would be well forever. Perhaps she had overcome my manipulation. If that were so, though, I could not help but feel she would have sent Lieutenant John Bridges to take him immediately to the scaffold. After the order was signed, there was no real reason to wait, was there? Yet, he was not dead. This gave me hope. Perhaps she would keep her promise. Or perhaps she did not have a choice.

My rooms high in the Tower were very stuffy, and for someone who was used to fresh air daily, it was exceedingly trying to be locked up thus. I pleaded with Sir John to release me into the gardens, and soon he submitted.

So, there I sat, on a stone bench admiring a little fountain, when I heard footsteps. I did not fear for my life, for there were several guards posted about, watching me at every second. However, as the footsteps came near, my heart began pounding in my chest for an unknown reason.

Trying to act inconspicuous, I leaned past a great tree to see down the path and almost fell off my bench. Robert was walking slowly toward me. He looked up from his feet and stopped dead when his eyes met mine. For a moment, his face was joy beyond anything I could believe, but then it changed to serious determination as his walking resumed, pointedly in my direction. Then he saw the guards and slowed again.

I did not know what to do. I wanted to race to him and embrace him. However, he was so deeply entrenched in plots against Mary that I could not show myself to be closely associated with him. Everyone knew that we had been tutored together and that we were friends, but no one knew that the friendship had remained and grown even stronger in adulthood.

His eyes never left me as he continued forward. He knew this garden well, for he maneuvered his way around the tree and slowly sat himself down a few yards from me on an adjacent stone bench. I wondered if he was allowed to come here often. He did not greet me... he did not touch me, or nod... he only looked into my face and I looked into his. We did not do anything else for several long minutes. I saw his emotions progress and change his countenance as he looked at me. I saw joy, disbelief, happiness, curiosity, confusion, fear, and finally anger.

Finally, he spoke, picking up our conversation where we left off the other night. "As long as she has you to teach her... help her see that she must not seek only her will... then..." He shrugged and bit his lip. "Honestly this is what I have always wanted, a way to permanently bind us together." His voice trembled a bit. "I just am grateful that you trust me to do this with you."

I had not known that I was holding my breath over this issue, but I had been. My hand rose as if to touch him and my face softened. But I stopped myself, looking around at the guards.

"It is a moot point."

He looked down at my stomach and shook his head, his eyebrows up in question.

I shook my head back at him.

He breathed in deeply as he tried to look relaxed on the bench, but I could see the stiffness in his motion and knew that he was restraining himself. Surveying the garden with a seemingly critical eye, he added, unable to stay restrained, "well, I suppose we will just have to keep on trying." A very small smile lifted the corners of his mouth and he looked at me askance.

I bit my lips together and stifled a laugh. "You will have no complaints from me, my good sir." And I sighed with anticipation and contentment. Then I looked up at this perfect, beautiful man that was mine and I felt my emotions begin to get the better of me. I felt as if I was not big enough to hold the love I had for him. "Robert," I whispered.

He'd watched this transition and reached for me, but did not finish, only said, "yes. I know."

Our eyes continued to keep the other's gaze until it was time for me to leave.

When my guard came close, Robert glanced angrily at him, then his eyes were back on me, his countenance changed. "Yes, my lady. The food here is awful. I hope they are treating you kinder than I, for you could well be this bungling lot's future queen."

"Well sir, let me remind you that the virtue of patience in one's trials is always a good lesson. Here is a chance to practice." I smiled and rose to follow my guard.

"Thank you for your wise words, dear princess. May the lord bless and keep you."

I turned to respond, but Robert pressed his hand to his chest. His fist over his heart, he clenched it there, his face a picture of beautiful fervor.

He loved me.

I nodded my head slightly, and covertly touched my fingertips to my lips before turning away.

I insisted on visiting the garden or walking the garden wall as often as I could. I needed the air, but I also was hoping to catch a glimpse of Robert again. It had been a week since our last visit and I had had no luck. I did, however, make friends with several little children who lived in the Tower with their parents. They played in the garden and along the wall. One day, a rather sweet little boy brought me flowers. He seemed taken with me. However, his offering did not go well with the council, for they kept me indoors for the next week, claiming that I could be receiving rebel messages from the children.

Infuriated by their unfounded distrust, I decided it was time to use my power. Besides, I could not be stifled, or I would go mad, and so would Kat and Blanche.

The light shown about me and I looked into Sir John's eyes the next time he was in my presence. "You will allow us to go outside for short periods of time each day."

I sent the light to him and he looked at me, confused, before saying, "yes, of course, my lady princess. I will let you outside each day, but under heavy guard and only for a few moments."

"For at least ten minutes." I flung the light with venom.

He nodded his acquiescence.

"Thank you, Sir John, may the Lord bless you for your kindness to us poor helpless women," I said and excused myself.

When I went back in my rooms, Lord William Paget sat with Kat awaiting my return. This man was a chameleon if I ever knew one. He worked for my father and Edward Seymour when he was in power over my brother. He had signed the settlement of the crown on Jane Grey and yet, here he was. Free. With a position in Mary's court. And I was in prison, though I had done nothing. Perhaps he had his own powers. Or perhaps I was not using mine as well as I might.

Lord Paget stood as I entered and, after a greeting, said hastily, "I do not have much time to tell you what I am about here, so I would beg of you to listen without question so that I may get through it all."

Confused at his manner, I nodded my head.

"Your highness, I would have you know why the queen will not see you. First, she is in a terrible state; if you only knew the fear and trepidation the rebellion caused in her, you would be forever forgiving. I do not think she will recover. She saw the rebels. They were right in front of her with their weapons of murder, and her with only a few incompetent guards to protect her. I fear, my lady, for her, the terror that engulfed her." I saw the false sincerity in him immediately. Though he might persuade others, a few weeks ago would have as easily seen my sister drawn and quartered and Jane the queen as he did give that speech.

Though, his words did make the bitterness of my own fear more real. I could truly empathize with Mary.

The slimy man went on. "She must have justice, my lady, and the reports coming in all point in your direction. Is it not understandable that she refuses to see you, and that she is so hard set on the subject?" I silently nodded, letting the man continue, for, insincere as he may be, he was giving me information I needed. "I would like to tell you what evidence is being brought about so that you may have time to prepare yourself. First, they have found evidence that you ordered arms to be made and discreetly collected at Donnington Castle."

I interrupted with great shock. "I never did!"

He raised his hand to cut me off and then went on, "they are squeezing Wyatt for all they can, but all he says is that he wrote you and that you responded with an oral message. He tells them that he planned to put you on the throne but that you never collaborated the plan. Also, somehow the French ambassador Renard has a copy of an obviously forged letter that has your name at the bottom. They are trying to prove that it was sent to the French ambassador, De Noailles, to gain French support. As soon as the rebellion was seen to be strongly backed by the people, cash, equipment, and troops, the French would intervene. Wyatt has admitted corresponding with De Noailles, and with his admitted correspondence with you… I am afraid it does not look good."

"But this proves nothing. You are telling me that they have no evidence. It is as I thought, all contrived. Of course, that is the only possible outcome, for I truly have done nothing against my sister the queen, and with no evidence, how can they keep me here? It is unlawful. Furthermore, my lord, why would one of Mary's council members be here to tell me this?"

"Because Emperor Charles has said he will not allow Regent King Philip across the channel until you, Lady Jane, and Wyatt are dead. The Queen did have other reasons for executing Lady Jane, but I do believe this threat her greatest motivator." He looked at the door anxiously, then turned back to me. "And I am here, a man who has followed his conscious when it was easy, but has now found himself too cowardly to die for those ideals, and have thus made a compact with the powers that be, though it damns my soul." He looked for the first time very contrite and righteously indignant toward his own self. "You see, I am a supporter of the Protestant cause. I am your man."

I straightened, not knowing exactly what to make of this man. "You were not so when Edward, may he rest in peace, was handing out crowns."

He looked even more disdainful at himself and would not meet my eyes. "No, I did not. It was a gamble John was certain he could win, and to my shame, I went along with it."

"It seems you have found your escape goat. I want no part of that. But I do thank you, sir, for the information. Still, I feel that this country would be better served if we all enlisted ourselves in the cause of unity, at least while we have a princess that cares for us and does what her conscious dictates her to do."

Lord Paget instantly went to his knees with a look of shocked admiration on his face. "You are the truest woman I have met, your highness. I am humbled by your loyalty. I am your man until death, but I will do as you so magnanimously suggest and honor my queen." Then he took my hand and kissed it before rising. "I must tell you this last before I go. Beware of Renard and Gardiner, they have the ear of the queen and constantly tempt her to get rid of you."

"Thank you, my lord. Your words will also be heeded, and I will be able to prepare myself more fully now. I thank you again." With that, he bowed himself out of the room.

I watched him go and wondered how I had won his admiration. Though he had done me a service today, he was not loyal, I would not forget. However, my thoughts were soon turned to my captors. I could not believe the audacity of those men. How could they, in good conscious, imprison and worse, kill, someone proven innocent?

I surrounded myself with light and let my mind plan not only a rebuttal, but a way to bring them to justice.

April 1554
Tower of London

I was completely shocked when Kat admitted to me that Sir John and Master Parry had discreetly routed arms and provisions to Donning-ton Castle. Kat said they had done so after I received the letter from Wyatt.

How had they known who that letter was from? Men knew so much more than they ever conceded, it seemed.

I knew now that they were acting to protect me, and I loved them for their loyalty and forethought. However, I would have them whipped for their blunder, if I had to wield the whip myself.

A month of my life wasted in the Tower. But then news came. Wy-att had confessed all in his long-awaited trial and was sentenced to death. It was only yesterday that the deed had been done. He had proclaimed for me and my innocence before they beheaded and quartered him. In a final act of degradation, his head was placed on top of the gibbet at St. James'.

It all seemed so primitively Roman that my stomach was sickened by it that whole morning. I wondered how much he had been tortured only to get him to admit my knowledge of the plot. I prayed for his soul and hoped he had not suffered too much on my account. However, I also knew that Mary had done what must be done, for he had led a very seri-ous rebellion and she had to keep civil peace.

I did not see Lord Paget again until I was called once more in front of the council. I wore a severe white dress and conducted myself as I thought a martyr would.

"Madam," Gardiner said, "we are here to ask you of the letter you wrote to the French."

"I would be happy to tell you all, if I had ever written such a letter," I interjected with the confidence of a princess.

"I have a copy of it right here."

"And why a copy my lord bishop? Where is the original? For that is not my writing." I watched their faces and then proceeded, "of course, how could it be, since I have never written such?"

I could see in Gardiner's eyes that he had very angrily given up on proving my guilt. He had nothing to charge me with and it rankled him. "What of the arms you had sent to Donnington Castle?"

"I will repeat myself and do so loudly, so all may hear me this time. I know nothing of Donnington Castle. If I had known of a rebellion, and I knew I had a fortified castle not far away, do you not think I would have hastened to it for my own protection? My lords, I am a simple-minded woman, can you not see that I would act in a way to protect myself if I had known I needed protection? This is all nonsensical and you all know it. I am innocent of any wrongdoing toward our beloved queen, and I will not continue to answer such foolish accusations." I played this up for all I was worth, my head high, my voice imperious, and I looked at them as my subjects.

Again, to my surprise, Gardiner rose and said in a quiet voice, "forgive me, your highness. I only do as I see best."

I nodded to him and he motioned for the guard to take me back to my rooms. I had again succeeded in convincing them of my innocence. God was blessing me… for, of course, it was the truth.

May 1554
The Tower of London

It was a beautiful spring morning and I walked through the Tower garden, my mind fully engaged. I had not had my courses last month, and though I did not think I could possibly be with child, I did not know what else to think. I felt no different. If this was true, I needed to tell Robert. Just so someone knew, for if Mary did not kill me—which day by day it looked more as if she would not—and Robert was not murdered, then... then we would have a child.

A chill raced up my back and I rung my hands and wondering what ever I would do.

When would I be set free? They had not questioned me in weeks, and I had heard how the trials of the traitors imprisoned with me had faired. Why was I not turned loose?

Recently, the guard had been drastically increased, and I wondered if Mary was going to use some other excuse to be done with me.

Interestingly, though there were more guards on the premises, my personal guard had been slackened. I did not know if this was Mary's order or if they just knew I would not try to escape, or if it was that there was a new constable, Sir Henry Bedingfield. He seemed to be a gentle sort of man, yet very straitlaced, and thus the perfect member of Mary's council. I doubted that they disagreed on anything.

As I thought and walked my path, I turned around a rather large budding oak. I rounded the edge of it and waiting on the other side—out of view of my guards—was Robert. Before I knew what was happening, he had pulled me to him and crushed me to his chest. Whispering in my ear, he said, "oh my darling, my only dreams have been of holding you in my arms." And then he had my face in his hands and was kissing me everywhere and pressing his cheek to my face.

My heart pounded at this happy surprise and I returned his love with eagerness. "Robert," I whispered back, kissing him, holding him.

We looked at one another, my hands clinging to his back and I felt that tears were coming.

"Do not cry, my love. Only walk around the tree as if you are examining it."

I knew what he was thinking, and it was good advice. It would perhaps buy us a few more seconds to be alone. I pulled my emotions together and did as he bade me. When the guard saw me, he stopped his advance. I took my time looking at the bark, admiring the budding branches, and then I was back in Robert's arms. "Do you have news of release?" he asked.

I looked at him with sadness. "I do not know. I cannot ask."

"Yes, I know. I fear to ask as well."

"I feel that I am almost at the end of this and just in time, too."

He wrinkled his brow. "In time? Do you have some pressing date I am unaware of?"

"Well," I said and pulled away from him, cradling my stomach. "I am fairly certain we have a pressing date."

His eyes blazed. His face turned white. "I thought…"

"I know. I as well. But like I said, I am not completely certain. However, I needed you to know, for there is planning that must be done. You will have to take the babe and claim it as your own, or some such excuse. For I will not be able to raise her, except as a very involved godmother."

With his face very pensive, he motioned for me to walk around the tree again.

I did so. But this time, I sat against the trunk where my guard could see me, but where I could also turn my face away and see Robert and talk without being noticed.

"This is not the time or place, but we do need to discuss it, my love," I said.

"Can you come to me again in the night?" he asked, his face very concerned now.

"I have waited for an opportunity every night and one has not come again. But I will keep trying. Lieutenant Bridges or Sir Bedingfield would have to come to me."

Robert thought. "Next time you see them, tell them they will come to you in the night."

I looked at Robert with adoration. "That is a brilliant plan. I never thought of doing that before. I wonder if it will work." I smiled at him and took his hand. "If it does, I will come as soon as I can."

He touched my face again, and this time he said, "I love you. Do you know how much I love you?"

"I am sure it equals my own love for you." And before I could do anything, he bent and kissed my lips… so gently… so sweetly.

"You should go."

"Yes, wait for me." I whispered and touched my finger to his lips once. My eyes held his eyes a moment longer, and then I stood and walked away.

My heart pounded as I doubled back to pass my guard.

May 1554
On the way to Woodstock, Oxfordshire

W hy am I to be taken to Woodstock, sir? And without the vital parts of my household? And under guard?" My voice rose with each question and seethed with irritation.

"Do not ask me questions, my lady, for there is nothing I can tell you until we arrive at our destination," Sir Henry Bedingfield repeated, as he had each of the five times I had previously canvassed the topic. "Look, see, your highness, we can see the castle in the distance; your waiting is almost done."

"Sir, this is nonsense. If I can see the castle then we have arrived, so tell me what I ask!" I hated idiocy and this man seemed to be made of nothing else. However, his attitude did tell me something of my situation, though his mouth truly had told me nothing.

I would be kept under some sort of house arrest, and Sir Henry Bedingfield was to be my keeper. It was evident that whatever his position was, he took it very seriously.

So, I was out of the Tower now, but away from Robert and my friends. Mary had decided to tuck me away, in a faraway place, so that I would be out from under her feet and out of the people's hearts and minds.

The five-day journey taught me why she did this; people cheered me and blessed me everywhere we stopped. Mary was very unpopular. Much of the people were converted to Protestantism and hated Mary's need to turn the ship around, so to say. They stood out for me by the dozens—how they knew where I was going when I did not even know was intriguing to say the least—and it was dangerous for them to do so. Somehow, I was loved, and it was interesting to watch my captors take that all in.

As strange and welcome as the adulation may be, it was also frightening, for I knew that if there were those with such passion one way, there certainly were enemies with equal zeal.

I finally realized the truth of my position, after situating myself in the drafty, ill-repaired gatehouse of a dilapidated hunting castle called Woodstock. I was still in prison, just of a different sort. Mary would not see me; thus I had to count on my earlier manipulations for myself and for Robert. And I was to have Robert's child. I felt the bud of growth in my womb and the tightness in my back and abdomen and the nauseous flurries in my stomach. Not to mention the headaches and ill tempers and dizziness and distaste for all things edible.

Besides all that, my gatehouse apartment seemed to be missing several essentials: Kat, Blanche, Robert, a nurse. But, paper and ink were the first non-human things I missed, for I wanted to write to Mary and tell her that this simply would not do. I was no threat to her. Straightway, I called my jailor, Sir Henry Bedingfield, to me.

"Sir Henry, I wish to write a letter, and it seems that I have no paper or ink in my rooms. I have not brought any with me, so I will require you to acquire some for me."

The fastidious fellow only addressed me on bended knee, so he looked up and swallowed hard. "I am sorry, my lady princess, my orders are that you are not to write or receive any letters." He saw my stunned expression and proceeded hurriedly. "Nor are you to have any visitors."

Anger washed over me like a raging sea of molten lava. "I have left the Tower! I am no prisoner. I cannot be held here without communication or visitation rights. I am a princess of England!" I was yelling by the end.

"Your highness, I plead with you to be understanding of my position. If we are to get along whilst under this roof, you must understand that I have my orders, and I will obey them to the fullest and with the passion of a loyal servant."

I understood and instantly felt ashamed for my anger toward him. "Yes, you are right. Forgive me." He nodded his head slightly and wiped his great brow with a handkerchief.

How could Mary do this to me, a beloved sister and princess of her kingdom? Lord Paget's words came back to me: Philip will not come unless you are dead. My sister needed a husband and heir much more than she needed a willful, blasphemous half-sister. "I understand perfectly what I must do," I said with an air of indignation. "You, I assume, are in contact with the council and the queen?"

"Yes, your highness, but I must be."

"I understand. Well, I suppose that I will just have to weary them with my cries for relief. Just like the woman from the scriptures who wearied her king until he became so tired of hearing her pleas, he gave in, only to get her to go away." I looked down at him. "And I am sorry to tell you this, but you might be the one who pays the price for the queen's orders." Clearing my throat, I said in a stately tone, "you will write to the queen and council and say that we arrived safely, but that I am much distressed by the accommodations. This drafty castle will lay us all in our graves by the time winter is upon us. Also, you will petition her to let me write to her majesty personally. Also, I would like to have Kat, Blanche, Lizzy, Sir John, and Master Parry returned to me at once, for I cannot function without them."

Sir Henry, who was still on his knees, paled. "I am sorry to inform you, your highness, but I can make but one of those requests. We will be staying here until the queen sees fit to move us, regardless of the castle's present condition. Moreover, your servants are… unfit examples for your highness. So, they will not be returning until they have proven to change their ways. Though I am keeping Master Parry at hand, for I cannot run all your business myself. I am not an educated man, at least not in the ways of a coffer." He then smiled up at me and continued, "I will mention to the council that you wish to write to the queen personally and we will see what they say." He rose and backed away. "Is that all your highness would have me write?" I did not speak for I was seething. "Well, then I will excuse myself and get to it." He left in quite a hurry. And it was a good thing too, for I found the nearest object and flung it in his direction. It was a vase which was made of copper, thankfully. Where this temper of mine came from, I had no idea.

But the information I now had about my surroundings made everything impossible. Was I to have my child all by myself? I worried and fretted, remembering Anna my maid at Hatfield and her violent end during birth. How was I to cope alone? What was I to do? I waded in the misery of my predicament for hours.

Finally needing some comfort, I pulled my power to me and instantly felt relief. Even hope. From another angle, this could not be better if it were planned out in the heavens. As it was, I had one maid – Dorothy – and one captor – Sir Henry – and a few guards. None I knew would be with me or be able to see me. How easy that would make it to hide my circumstance. I was sure I could manipulate Sir Henry and Dorothy until January, making sure they did not notice my changing body. Nor, when my child would come. I might even be able to manipulate Sir Henry to write to Robert. I wanted to force him to let me write to Mary, but I had learned to take responsibility for my actions. Mary might imprison or kill Sir Henry for such a breach and, though I was not his friend, I knew a good and loyal subject when I met one. Sir Henry Bedingfield was the most loyal of men and did not deserve punishment. But Robert… I might never know if he got word to Robert. Of course, this all hung on Robert being released from the Tower.

My mind took the scheme even further; with as little attention as I got, Robert could even live here with me and no one would be the wiser. Then he could take our child and do with her as we arranged. This could be a very clean affair.

I felt the first thrill and gratitude for my circumstance and began to construct the circumstances in my mind. I only had to make sure Mary stayed angry with me until then, and fortune would bless me and my child. What would annoy her but not put her over the edge of wanting to be rid of me? Religion was the most important thing to Mary, or so she said; however, I felt it was her pride. She wanted to turn back the clock and make sure all knew how ill-treated she and her mother had been. As long as I did not prick her pride, nor acted against her religion, I would not make a mortal mistake. I needed to act the spoiled brat she thought I was. Well, I was off to a great beginning. As long as Mary could torture me, just a little bit, she probably would be happy. I needed only to keep complaining and requesting things she would not give me. That would make her happy and help her feel she was powerful.

A part of me, filled with the light of my power, considered the feeling I had that first night I went to Robert—the night I'd conceived—how my guard with mine and Robert's keys had been right there, in the night, in a spot I could call to him. How easy it all had been.

It made me wonder, was a mightier hand than mine guiding me?

I could not focus all of my time trying to aggravate Mary and keep my secret under wraps, for I had a thorn in my side and his name was Sir Henry Bedingfield. I was not entirely sure what station this man had in my household. He forbade me anything I wanted with the ease and air of authority only a parent or a king would assume.

When I asked to ride my horse, he simple replied, "I have heard that you were a great rider, but I am sorry your highness, it is out of the question. That activity is too... volatile and freeing. I am sorry, I do have my orders."

When I asked for books, he was "not qualified to ascertain if they were appropriate for my situation." And thus, would have to send the titles off to the council to be judged. Though this was annoying, I took a bit of pleasure in sending off to the council many, many books to be judged. I did everything in my power to make him and the council miserable with a constant stream of demands.

When I demanded tutors, instruments for study, or music to annoy

Mary, he would say, "no, your highness, I am sorry, but I have my orders. Those requests are impossible at this time."

It was a complete contradiction. He would kneel before me and call me your highness, yet deny me everything, like I was a child of five and asking to race a chariot.

He, an ill-educated country gentleman, deprived of me everything and anything I wanted. It burned in me like nothing ever had.

Furthermore, to add fuel to that fire, I was told I was responsible for him. I had to take care of his living expenses, as well as to pay him monthly. I... I was his employer, for he was to take Master Parry's place for now. Inconceivable!

And as for Master Parry, I took a house for him in Woodstock township and paid him his salary as if he were working for me. Before long, I had all the vital members of my house lodging at the Bull Inn. And work for me they did. Sir Henry would let me communicate with Master Parry here and there, and it was through him I realized the bulk of world news, for I was without any communication from the outside world. Even the guards, who constantly surrounded the gatehouse, did not speak to me. Christ himself may have come in all his glory and there I would be, alone, at Woodstock.

I needed to know Mary's comings and goings and intrigues. I needed to know about Robert. I needed to know about my friend, William Cecil, etcetera.

I, of course secretly—and blatantly—sent Dorothy into town with verbal messages for Master Parry and the others. Most importantly, I needed to know the mood of the people. How were they handling my imprisonment? Did they know I was imprisoned? What was taking the council so long to respond to Sir Henry's letters?

Intrigue is a form of entertainment when there are none others to be had, and it caused me to set up a method of conveying secrets, should I need it in the future.

~

Through my sources, I found out that Mary's marriage with Spain was back on. Though she had promised the people in London who would support her through the rebellion that she would never marry a foreigner, it was all forgotten now.

Needless to say, Phillip was highly unpopular, and I was glad to hear that people were speaking out about Mary's broken promise; though those who did found themselves in prison more often than not. Mary would have her way, for it was ordained by God for her to have a catholic husband. I had dreamt this. I saw her. Angry vengeance raining down on the heads of the Protestants. Questioning many and hurting them for their beliefs. It was a wispy dream and I knew that meant her path was not yet certain, yet still I feared for my countrymen and friends.

June 1554
Woodstock Oxfordshire

I felt my child move within me. She fluttered like a moth. I think I could not love anything but Robert as much as I love her.

July 1554

Woodstock Oxfordshire

Mary married Phillip of Spain at Winchester Cathedral. I was not invited.

If only I could see Mary for ten seconds, this would all be over with. I would manipulate her and then proceed as a free woman, manipulating any on her council who desired to see me in chains again. I knew I could do it now, for I was so experienced manipulating every day, that I was sure I could control fifty men at once. How frustrating it was to have so much power and not be able to use it.

That was my selfish nature. I wanted to be a part of the festivities. I wanted to be a part of my only sister's wedding.

But I had a child to think about now. So, I would have to forgo many things.

.

August 1554
Woodstock Oxfordshire

Time drug on and on. The hot summer passed, and my belly began to swell. By August, I was halfway through with my pregnancy and had to continually use my power to manipulate Dorothy, who bathed me and dressed me and took out my chamber pot. I had never spent so much time using my power. I had to keep it pulled to me every moment, just in case. Luckily, I carried the babe well and did not need new dresses yet, though I stopped wearing a corset as soon as I moved into Woodstock, for what was the point? Sometimes for days and days, the only person I saw was Dorothy.

I felt it was time to implement some plans. Fortune touched me and one day Dorothy mentioned that her mother, Dena, was a nurse maid. As soon as I heard these words, I knew that it was a sign. I questioned Dorothy minutely about her mother and was satisfied by the report. I called Sir Henry to me and told him that I needed Dena as my lady. I liked older women better, Dorothy was a good girl, but I needed someone more experienced.

This seemed a reasonable thing to Sir Henry, and he inquired if a change would be appropriate. The council took no issue, and after I explained to Dorothy that I had other work for her to do. She was glad of the matter, no doubt tired of my company and longing for better employment. I told her to go to Master Parry with instructions.

With one obstacle faced, I only waited for Robert.

My other plan—to keep Mary annoyed with me—started a new chapter as well. I knew Mary would loathe explaining herself. It would bring all the angers to the forefront and make her keep me longer. So, I put my foot down and demanded Sir Henry discover on what grounds I was being imprisoned.

"Life in the Tower was better than this," I complained angrily to him, "for at least there, I knew my place. At least I had my friends near me. So, if I am not a prisoner and I am not free, what am I? I have been charged of no crime. I have not been tried or convicted of anything. Why am I here? I demand to know!" I pointed to the table and said, "I will have no more excuses. I will have no more dillydally. You will write these questions at once to my sister, the queen, and send them this very day."

"I am very sorry..." Henry started, but I cut him short.

"Sir Henry, I pay your wages. I am your mistress besides being your princess. You will do as you are commanded!"

He wrote and was as direct in his questioning of the queen as I could make him be.

The letter was passed into the hands of the courier, and I began marking the days to see how long it took to get a reply. One thing about house arrest: I was beginning to be very good at waiting.

It took ten days. But I did not waste that time. Dorothy was off with Master Parry, hopefully inquiring about Robert and finding a property Robert and our child could stay in after he took our child—the crown had confiscated all his property as a traitor. Dena was now my maid and learning my ways. I tried something with her I never thought of trying before. I told her about the child and manipulated her to keep quiet about it. This way, she was prepared, and I had a woman of experience to talk to about the birthing bed. And talk we did. Amazing, frank conversations of the kind I'd never had before. I locked us in my rooms and did not let the woman go until I had every last detail from her. Dena, the blessed woman, had worked on my dresses as we talked. She'd taken out many of the hems and added random scraps of material to others, which looked preposterous. However, it did not matter, for there was no one to see me.

I was so grateful to Dena for all her many services, that I swore to take care of her always.

When the letter from Mary came, I was not allowed to read it. Sir Henry was kind enough to give me the details, though.

He bustled into the room excited, and I almost forgot to manipulate him to only look at my face, for my belly was very noticeable now, and that was how I'd gone about things with him. I was getting so good at it, I did not actually have to say the words out loud, I could just think them. I didn't even have to gesture.

He took his notes from his pocket and began telling me my sister's reply. I listened carefully, but not until he said that I was allowed to write to her, was I interested.

I instantly demanded paper and pen, which I was given, and then proceeded to list my complaints. I aimed them purposefully to annoy, not infuriate.

My dear sister and queen,

I hope you are in good health and that your position is bringing you happiness and peace.

I am grateful to you that I have been let out of the Tower, but I must ask what position I am in now. I am not accused of anything; and I am not to be tried any further. I do not think it is lawful for you to hold me a prisoner when I have done nothing wrong. I swear to you I am innocent of any malicious act against you. If you have found something to accuse me of, please do, and bring me before you so that I might defend myself. I have not had the great pleasure of seeing you since last November when I stood for you in the struggle for the crown. I would dearly love to be brought forth so that I might show my loyalty and humility.

Furthermore, the conditions of this castle are hardly befitting a sister of the queen. It is in ill repair and is drafty and cold. Could not repairs be done before the winter, if I am to stay here?

I would also like to ask why I am not able to ride my horse. This is not at all correct treatment, for I desperately need the exercise.

Though I have my own money to buy them, I need to ask for some new clothes. For Sir Henry tells me I cannot even see a seamstress. Sister, this is too much! No clothes? You might as well take my food, though I am paying for that too, here in my prison.

I would still love to have my books so that I can exercise my mind, for I fear it is getting dull stuck here without anything to nurture it. And some music would be a great comfort.

Please see to it that Sir Henry knows that I am to be obliged in these matters, for he is highly fastidious, and if you do not say it plainly, he will not know your meaning.

Your loyal servant,
Elizabeth

"That should do it," I said, and folded the letter. Sir Henry took it and read it. The impertinence of the man! "What right have you to read my letter? Am I always to be laid naked before you, sir?"

He blushed thoroughly. "I am only following orders. I find this line… and that one, a bit impertinent, your highness." He pointed the lines out. "Please fix them before we send it off."

"I will not," I said with venom. "I said what I wanted to say. Or did the queen give you instructions on how I was to word my letters?"

"As a matter of fact, she did. I am to make sure that you do not offend."

"I will not offend her unless she feels guilty about something. If I am here under correct pretenses, then she has nothing to be offended about." I, once again, had tied this man's wits in knots and, once again, it did me no good.

"It will be fixed as I say, or I will not send the letter."

Leaving the letter on the desk, I stood and walked away from him without a word. My heart pounded, and I desired very much to use my power on the man to make him see my way, but this was a matter of pride. I did not need to change my words to my own sister.

Drama is a fierce weapon. If done correctly and in duration, it can be as useful as any sword, or pen for that matter.

The drama I put on for Sir Henry's benefit would have made Master Boushe, our dance instructor, proud. Needless to say, several weeks of sickness and temper tantrums had done nothing. The man was loyal to a fault, and truly, I admired him for it.

My letter was toned down to his satisfaction and then sent off.

Still, Mary was not happy with me, or with Sir Henry. In her responding letter, she reviewed all of the charges that she had laid at my door in March. Though there had been no evidence, she insinuated that it did not matter what I said, she believed the evidence to be the truth, and thus was treating me with more clemency and favor than usual for traitors, on account of my previous support. Furthermore, I was not allowed to weary the council anymore unless I could compose myself as if I were talking to God, thus bespeaking the proper respect.

I smiled inwardly at this. I had done what I wanted and definitely gotten under her skin. Oh, I would tell Sir Henry to write for me again, for this was actually fun.

November 1554
Woodstock Oxfordshire

One request Mary did acquiesce to was that we hold mass in Woodstock chapel and that I attend alone. She did not want the people to get at me any more than I wanted people to see me, though our reasons were not the same. With my extreme belly and mismatched dresses, I looked a vagabond.

Still, I attended mass nearly every day. It was something to do, but it was not enough to convince Mary that I had converted.

My spirit was low through the autumn months, for I had been under house arrest for over half a year. I missed my love, and my friends. Not even my small intrigues and the bits of gossip the servants brought livened my spirit.

Sleep was ruined because of my child rolling within me. Food was a bother. I could not even convince myself to get angry and begin a yelling spree. Boredom and discomfort were the theme of my life; in fact, I had taken a motto to myself: "semper eadem." Always the same. And it was.

However, one brisk day in November, as I sat in my room, Dorothy entered with a light in her eyes that told me she had news from Master Parry. She had been a source of information. I was already surrounded with my light and thus quickly manipulated her to not notice my figure.

Obediently, her eyes went to my face and stayed there.

"What is it? What has happened?" I said with forced vigor.

"My lady, your sister, the queen, is pregnant."

My mind instantly saw what this could mean, and my spirits lifted. "Is it certain? She is so old?" Perhaps I would be set free now, for with a child in the succession before me, I could no longer be seen as a danger.

"Yes. She has all the signs, and the doctors say the child will come in May."

I placed a hand over my own extended belly. "Well, I am happy for her." It only took a moment for my mind to conjure how frightening this could be. What if, in her joy, she released me?

"There is more, my lady. Master Parry said you might find it interesting that Robert Dudley and his brothers have been released from the Tower. I believe he said that his brother-in-law, Henry Sidney, got in good with King Philip and he saw that it was done."

I swallowed hard and sat up, sending a prayer of thanks to God for his mercy. Robert! And in the nick of time. "Thank you, Dorothy, this is exactly what I waited for. Please, thank Master Parry, should you happen upon him again. All of his news has been well received."

Without hesitation, I enacted my plan. Summoning a ball of power, I said, "Dorothy, take your slip off."

Once it was done, I took it and tossed it to her mother. "Open the waist big enough to fit a small piece of paper."

"Dorothy, send for Sir Henry and while he is with me, go get a pen and paper from Sir Henry's study. Now! Tell no one and do not get caught." Balls of light accompanied the commands.

"I will, my lady." She said, and bowed her way out.

I did not have to wait long, because it was Sir Henry who opened the outer door of my chambers for Dorothy's exit. The girl was wise enough to not say that I wanted to speak with him. She only left.

"Come, Sir Henry." I said, and simultaneously flung light in his eyes to not look at my figure. My heart was beating quickly, and I could not stop looking at the door for Dorothy.

When he came, I pretended that Mary's pregnancy was a surprise, but he also told me that Mary had reinstated Cardinal Pole as Archbishop of Canterbury and that England was back in good graces with Rome. He fidgeted as he said, "Parliament has also reinstated the law against heretics."

I barely knew what to say, so I stumbled through, "so... anyone suspected of... of heresy or, as Mary will see it, Protestant beliefs, will be what...?"

"Burned at the stake, your highness," he said with real sorrow. It seemed I was already condemned in his mind and he was sad about it. His heart had turned toward me. That was good.

I swallowed hard. I knew that I had a long list of grievances in Mary's mind, and the charges surrounding Wyatt's rebellion were only some of my supposed traitorous deeds. At the top of her list was that I was a Protestant in my heart, and she knew it. No matter how I acted, she knew. "I cannot believe that Mary would take such a strict stance. This must be the influence of King Philip and the new cardinal."

"I know not, my lady. What I do know is that I have seen you go to mass every other day for months now. That is all I will include in my reports to the council, should they ask. Your behavior has been impeccable since you stopped sparring with me in every circumstance, and so I will also be mentioning that. I am loyal to the queen, but I do not see that she has anything to fear from you now that she is with child, no matter your innocence or guilt."

I had to grimace inside. Sometimes I wondered if the man knew what came out of his mouth. "I thank you, sir, but I will say that I am offended that you are not convinced of my innocence in earnest. I have done nothing wrong toward my sister; I do not even talk badly of her, though she has treated me thus. I attend mass and say my prayers and feel the sting of my sins most profoundly. What must I do to prove myself?" I rose and started pacing the room in an irritation I did not fully understand. "If you, who has lived with me and watched me at every moment, cannot believe, why do I insist on writing to her or seeing her?

The cause is lost. I will die an innocent traitor."

I truly did feel horrid, but I needed Sir Henry to believe me; I do not know why, but I did.

"Your highness, do not take it thus," he said, and rushed to pat my arm. "You are as good as can be. Do not fret."

This country man had proven to me what good stock he was and, though I was completely annoyed by his fastidious nature, he had put up with my tantrums and manipulations as a saint would. It was a sign that I was broken down that I was feeling thus for my jailer.

In my mind, I blamed it on the pregnancy and the overwhelming thoughts of Robert.

Dorothy came back not five minutes after Sir Henry left. She had what I needed. I quickly wrote two notes.

Robin- I am at Woodstock manor in the gatehouse under strict house arrest. All windows of the southwest corner of the second floor are mine. Knock at them and ye shall be received. We are waiting for you. Bessy

Master Parry- Do not ask me how I am writing you. Luck is all I can tell you. I need this note to get to Robert Dudley. It is very important. I promised Robert I would help him financially since my sister confiscated his possessions. So, send money for travel, he has not seen his wife in almost a year. Also, please do everything you can to keep it private and immediate. E.T

Once the ink dried, I folded the scraps and Dena sewed them into Dorothy's skirt, for all visitors were searched.

I manipulated the ladies. "You will take these notes to Master Parry. You will not think of it again after you complete this task."

I had to make sure I always manipulated these two together, for if someone learned of what I was doing, I did not think it would work on them any longer. Like with Robert and my father.

I sent them on their way and breathed. Robert. Robert was to come to me.

Woodstock was upwards of seventy miles from London. That is five days hard riding for the courier, and then time for the man to find Robert, and then a five-day ride back for Robert. Ten to twelve days until I would see my love, if the stars were with me and all went well. I was beyond excited. I had waited so long, a week and a half seemed like nothing.

It only took Robert four days total.

I lay in my bed, almost asleep, when I heard a click, click, click on the window next to my bed. I rolled over like a huge ball, wondering at the sound. Then I heard it again on the next window down. I could not imagine what it could be, so I arose and, with a candle in hand, went to the glass. The moon was out, but I noticed the steam of breath in the cold first. And then my love stepped through the mist and I saw him, and he saw me.

I began trembling and could not unhook the latch at the window. Finally, the job was done. I leaned out. Tears now in my eyes, my mouth smiling as wide as could be. I reached toward him. "My love," I whispered.

He all but clambered up the stone wall to get to me, to touch my hand. "Go to the door, wait for me there," I whispered to him.

He nodded.

I ran from my room, as well as I could with my child inside me. When I reached the door guard, I cast him aside with a ball of light and I flung the doors wide.

Robert emerged from the bushes and did not race to my side as I wished. He walked toward me slowly, taking me in. My pregnant belly, my light-shrouded figure in a nightdress. My red hair blowing with the winter breeze.

I took two steps out of the door in my bare feet, my arms extending and aching to hold him.

He seemed to catch my meaning and stepped faster until he was in my arms. He felt like perfection and he smelled like horse and sweat and

Robert. I held him so tight, I could not feel the cold.

"My love," he whispered into my hair, "should we not go in? I fear for the child."

I pulled away slightly and, after a glance at my face, he looked toward my belly, placing a hand on our child. After a solemn moment, he looked back into my eyes and took my face in his hand, pressing our foreheads together.

I took him by the shoulders and pulled him inside. He shut the doors and glanced at the two guards staring at their feet.

"What did you do to them?" he whispered.

"I told them not to look."

He blinked at the men and then at me. "For how long?"

I shrugged. "Forever."

His face went into shock.

I bit my lip and giggled, then shook my head. "They will be right as rain in the morning."

"Except a crick in the neck."

I pulled him away. "I will tell them to get over that tomorrow."

He followed me, and we moved quickly to the kitchen. He looked at me, confused.

"You smell."

"Oh, that's the thanks I get for my trouble."

"You will get plenty of thanks, once you are clean," I said with an arched eyebrow.

Robert licked his lips and his head tilting to the side. "I have missed you terribly."

I placed a finger over his lips. "Shh, just take your clothes off."

He did as he was told and stripped to his skin and, though he was dirty, I could not help but touch him with concern. He was no longer the beautiful stallion of a man that I remembered. The glorious physique I admired was all but wasted away.

"I will hurt Mary for not feeding you!" I swore.

"I will not stop you. Why feed someone you are going to kill? If not for my sister's husband, I might not be here."

I touched his chest with murder for my own sister in my heart. "I suppose we both have different forms at present."

"Yes, but Elizabeth, let us talk after I am dressed. I am freezing."

The large pot of water over the almost-dead fire was still quite warm, so we used it. Working together, we got him cleaned up quickly. I was always surrounded by light now, and used my power to pull all the water droplets from his skin, and made them race across the floor and out the larder door. I proceeded to take his rough traveling garments and dunk them in the pot. I had never done wash before, but I did know the process. There was no lye soap about, that I could find, but I could aggravate the water with my power. I forced that water to rage and roil in the pot like a hurricane, but I did not let one drip fall to the floor. After several minutes, I thought perhaps they would be clean and had Robert hold them up. I could not tell, so I pulled all the water out of them and he examined them.

"They are as good as can be expected."

I smiled and sniffed. "They're slightly better at least."

He put them back on and I told the water in the pot to follow the same path as the other, out the larder door. I felt bad that the cooks would not have any hot water in the morning, but there was nothing to be done about it.

"You are so incredible. I know that sounds trite, but what else am I supposed to say?"

"Thank you, I know." I smiled at him. "Now grab some food, and a lot of it, for I intend on feeding you properly."

There were a few apples left, and some scones and hard cheese and breads. He found the smoked joint of a hog and sliced off a goodly portion.

We smuggled all up to my rooms.

Once there, we gravitated toward the fire, which had thankfully not gone out. Robert stoked it and laid several more logs on.

I pulled a shawl around me, eased into a chair, and asked, "are you planning on a long night? That's a lot of wood."

Robert turned from his chore, his eyes roaming my face languidly. Then he put the poker away and knelt at my feet. His hand lifted, his fingertips floating just above my cheek, his eyes provocatively still searching me. "Elizabeth, my love," he whispered, and his face crumpled. There was pain there, there was longing there, there was a fire.

I leaned toward him and gripped his face. "I will make all right, I swear it to you."

He shook his head. "There is no making this right. Elizabeth. I only want to move forward. With you, with our child." My hands slid to his shoulders, as he gently cupped my belly. "My mother had many children and I fear she did not carry them as well as you. It begs the question; is all well and right with you and the child? If my calculations are correct, she is due in about ten weeks? I feel as if your belly should be quite a lot bigger."

Shocked, I chided, "Robert Dudley! You impertinent man."

He smiled his beautiful roguish smile. "There you are. I love it when you call me impertinent. I want to know how the child fairs. How my love fairs. I cannot help impertinence. I will know everything, my sweet, for I have lost so much already." He took my shoulders and looked seriously into my eyes. "I do not want to be separated from you ever again."

"Nor I from you."

He pulled me to him in an awkward hug and he felt like joy and smelled like Robert. It did not take long for me to desire more of him, so I pulled away. "Are you ever going to kiss me, husband?"

He looked longingly at my mouth, and wet his own full, perfect lips. "I will admit I want to so badly it might be doing me bodily harm."

"Well then," I whispered. "What are you waiting for?"

He groaned. "My darling, I fear to start. I..." He blushed and sat back on his heels, a hand rubbing at his scruffy face, unable to look at me now.

"Robert!" I said in a demanding tone. "Speak."

He smiled and raked his hands through his curls, but began slowly to talk. "I am in a bit of a delicate condition my dear, and so are you. I fear that my long absence from you will overwhelm me, and in the passion of our kiss, I will not act as I should."

My mind flitted over these words, trying to make sense of them. I did not know much about men, not really, but I did know that they reportedly had a much stronger desire for all that was carnal. However, I could not imagine how his desire could be stronger than mine, for it took all my willpower to control it when he was near. I even felt overwhelming stirrings of this nature in my present condition, round and large as I was. In fact, just the thought of being with my husband filled my body with excitement and warmed me almost to a boil.

"Robert if you do not kiss me and do all manner of indecent things to me this very night, I might never talk to you again."

Robert's jaw opened in shock. He blinked at me and leaned further back on his heels, unable to believe I meant what I said. I stared him down, as serious as can be, and when he stayed motionless—except his breath coming faster and his pupils becoming larger—I broke the spell by whispering, "Robert, do not worry. I will be perfectly fine and so will the child. Please take me. I can wait no longer."

With infuriating slowness, Robert stood, and with hand outstretched, pulled me to my feet. Once I was standing, he took my face in his hands and slowly, gently leaned down. Our lips met in a sweet, luxuriant kiss, which molded and moved and tied my heart and brain and body into a mess of desire and overwhelming love and longing and loss.

I sighed and enjoyed every movement of his lips on mine. I forced myself to stay in the moment and not push more passion upon him just to speed up the process. He pulled me to the couch, where he sat, and I moved on to his lap. Then we made up for all the kisses we had missed while apart, whispering in between how we loved one another and admired one another and missed one another. It was perfect.

As the fire quieted into a nice steady burn, and my mouth began to be bruised I told him it was time to move to the bed and he agreed.

Morning came, and Robert still lay in my bed, his arms around me cradling my stomach like the most perfect dream. But the third member of our little family wanted to make her presence known. She began kicking and fighting against the heavy man arms that squished her space.

Robert's head came up. "Is that her? That... that is my child wiggling around inside of you."

His mussed hair and sleepy eyes forced me to roll over for a better look at him. I loved his face more than anything in this world. The soaring heights of cathedral arches did not stand against Robert in all his glory. The awe of the white cliffs at Dover was nothing to the awe I felt knowing he loved me.

I brushed his lips with my bruised ones and let him feel Anne punching and twisting inside me. I had named my child after my mother in my head.

After she settled down, I spoke. "We have so much to discuss. Like how in the name of heaven did you get here so quickly? I only heard you were released four, well now five days ago."

"Easy. You may have heard that, but I was released over two weeks ago."

I sat up. "Really?"

"It took me a few days to procure your whereabouts. At court, Mary keeps discussion of you stifled. Though my brother-in-law, Henry, who is quite in the new king's favor, gained the information. I wasn't astonished that Mary was keeping you prisoner, but where was a surprise. It is a journey, as you well know. Henry also lent me a horse and some capital. I came as quickly as could be; however, the horse was not the steed I needed and thus, I had to let him rest far too often." He pulled me closer and slung a leg over mine. "So, you see, my darling, I was on my way to you. Always on my way to you." One elbow held him up and the other snaked out from between the blankets to brush a curl back from my cheek.

His eyes tracing my face, his lips came down to meet mine.

I could kiss this man forever. With any luck, I would get to.

He pulled back a smile on his face. "You will not believe this, but the courier Master Parry sent for me was a man familiar with me and my family. We passed on the road not ten miles outside of Woodstock. He recognized me and was able to give me your message and the funds. I was so relieved, for I had no idea what I would do once I arrived. I knew Mary was keeping you with guards." He traced my face with a fingertip, and I felt goose flesh rise up all over my body. He laughed to himself, "I had fantasies of charging in and defeating the guards and racing to your side."

I smiled back to him, imagining the scene he described. I turned to press my body against his and wrap my arm around his chest. "Of course, you did. You are my lord. My protector. The captain of my heart. The keeper of my body. You came for me."

"And you preformed the impossible to aid me."

I pulled him tighter. "It is not impossible if you are what I am."

"No, I do not think anything is impossible for you, my love."

He dipped his head to kiss me. Softly at first, and then his passions overwhelmed him, and I let them take me away as well.

We sat languidly by the fire the next morning discussing plans for the future, when my maid entered to stoke the fire. Robert, being the gentleman he was, stood to get out from underfoot, but he frightened Dena out of her skin and had to grab her so that she did not back into the flames.

I quickly spoke to sooth the situation. "Dena, it is alright. It is my dear friend, Robert Dudley. Robert, this is Dena. She and her daughter, Dorothy, are my loyal maids. Dena is also a midwife and will be assisting me. Dorothy will be the one who goes with you when…" I stumbled over my words, not wanting to think about what must happen to my child, "…when it becomes necessary."

"Dena." Robert said and bowed slightly to her. "It is good to meet you."

She nodded and curtsied. "Thank you, my lord." But she looked to me, uncertain of what to make of the circumstances.

I pulled the light to me and spoke, "Robert will be staying here with me. You will not speak of him in any way to anyone, ever."

The large ball of light hit her, and her face went blank. "Yes, my lady." And she went back to stoking the fire.

I looked at Robert. He was staring at me, of course. He always did when I was surrounded by light.

He whispered, "And that is enough? She will not say anything?"

"Yes." I whispered back. "I could tell her to simply not notice you. That is what I do with everyone about this." I added and pointed to my belly. "I have to do it to everyone I see. Thankfully, since I am imprisoned, that is not very many people. Honestly, I could not have planned this better myself. It is as if it were written in the stars." I smiled at him and rubbed my belly.

I saw his face soften and, as he looked at me and our child, his emotions got the better of him. He placed a hand over his face and I instantly looked to Dena. "That will be all, Dena. I would like breakfast for two in half an hour. Just tell cook I find myself terribly hungry. I will deal with her later."

Dena nodded and moved to the door as I moved to Robert.

I knelt before him and rubbed his leg. "What is it?"

It took him a moment to whisper. "It is not... I just..." he sighed, "I am grieving."

This took me by surprise. "For what?"

He moved his hand and his azure eyes were sparkling with tears, his dark lashes wet. "For us. For all that could have been. For all the hardship we face. But also..." He wiped at his face, feeling embarrassed. He straightened in his seat and cleared his throat. "I am probably just in a weakened state. As you well know, I have been in prison for over a year, starved, questioned, and damaged. In that time, my father and Guildford were murdered. My other brother, John, who was sick coming out of prison, could also be dead. I have no idea how he fairs. He had an infection of the lungs. It was bad. I pray to God that he is well. My mother is not in great health, nor is..." he paused and looked up at me, "Amy, whom I do not love, but am responsible for, nonetheless. All of my possessions were seized, and I have no idea what has become of her. To my utter shame, I did not even ask after her when I was released."

I turned away at this, but only for a moment as my mind acknowledged that this was one of the reasons I loved Robert so deeply. He was a kind and caring soul, loyal, and one who did not shirk responsibility.

I thought it through. Robert had come to me immediately. He came to rescue me. Fortunately, or rather, unfortunately, I did not need rescuing. I was well. It was fully selfish for me to keep him for two months when his life outside these walls was falling apart. Besides, what would I do with him here? He would have to stay confined in my room, for I could not control every eye in the world. He would be spotted. It was a dangerous game we played.

I sat straighter and spoke. "Well, I am as selfish as a creature can be, and I will not allow you to leave for at least a few more days, but I do understand your distress for your family, your livelihood and your... Amy." I sniffed. "This obligation you feel is one of the many things I love about you. It will make you a wonderful father," I said and grasped his shirt to pull him toward me. "Just promise me you will be back before the new year."

His face softened again, and he kissed me so softly, so lovingly. "I promise," he whispered and kissed me again. "Thank you for understanding."

I pulled away from yet another kiss and put my features in a serious expression. "But listen here, Robert Dudley, I will not be pleased if you miss the birth of our child."

"Speaking of that, I have my part of our plan to work out as well. Our daughter needs a home and I have none at the moment. Still, I will move heaven and earth to be here, my love." He pushed me gently backward on the carpet, supporting my head as I lay back. Then he lay next to me. "I love you," he whispered and traced my cheekbone with a feather-light fingertip. "The road ahead is a treacherous one. I foresee much hardship for us. Much separation. Much hiding. But I need you to know, that I know our love can weather the storms. I would do it all again, because it was the way I got you. You are a joy to me like nothing else. You captivate me. You amaze me, always. You truly are my world, Elizabeth."

Robert and I spent a wonderful few days in my rooms, loving each other, talking non-stop and scheming. We figured out a plan for our child.

The gist of it was hard but the only way. Our daughter would live with Robert and Amy when Mary let me go. But, in order for that to happen, Robert had to get his property back from Mary. Henry Sidney, Robert's brother-in-law, was connected to the king and had invited Robert to attend a tournament hosted by King Phillip with the hope that Robert could court the monarchs favor, and perhaps prove himself an ally to my sister. If he could do that, she would give his land and titles back to him. Our plan depended on it. The tournament was to be held in seven short days and would be over before the Christmas season began. So, it was decided that Robert would attend. He would leave in the morning and, if all went well, would stay for an entire month.

Our backup plan, should Mary prove stubborn, would be so much more difficult for me. I would get Kat and Sir John near enough that I could manipulate them into thinking the child was theirs for a while. It would be near impossible, for Kat was not even on this side of the country at present. And I honestly didn't know if I would be strong enough to live with my daughter when she could not be my daughter, nor strong enough to torment Kat that way.

When all was as ready as it could be, I fell into Robert's arms, loving him and fretting over the loss of him for an entire month, for I knew he would mesmerize Mary as he had done me and Kat and everyone else who knew him.

I watched Robert ride away in the dead of night and cried myself to sleep.

January 1555
Woodstock Oxfordshire

Robert had triumphed. Mary had not made it official, but Robert had done well at the tournament. He got me a letter through Dena, something we set up before his leave taking. His friendship with the king was certain and strong, and Mary skeptically and begrudgingly agreed with Phillip.

Now, all that needed was for the child to come. I could admit to myself that I was very fearful, regardless of Dena's calming words and reassurances that all women from our Mother Eve had born children.

Still, I would wake up with sweats from terrible dreams. I would worry and fret all the day long. I could not eat, nor sleep. The image of my long-dead maid repeated over and over, blood, death. Her remembered screams lingered in my ears.

I questioned Dena to the point of violent annoyance, I am certain. But I could not help it. I was frightened. So much could go wrong. I did not want to die.

The night before Robert's expected arrival, I began to have pains. Dena told me that though I was not due for several more weeks, she was sure that the baby would be coming sooner than that.

"Is that alright? Is it normal?" I asked.

"Yes, of course, my dear. God decides when it is the proper time for babies to come, and we can do nothing to change it. Come rest now, you'll need it if this baby comes tomorrow."

"Tomorrow!" I shrieked, for it could not be.

The night progressed on and, though the pains worsened, I thankfully was able to get some sleep. I even felt a little excitement. However, when the morning came, I was no longer excited. I was very much in pain. My stomach would tighten and loosen in a measured pace, like my body was keeping time to an excruciating dance.

In between bouts of pain, Dena cursed that she needed four hands as she did busy work. She boiled water and collected rags and bedding as I began to sweat and to feel very light-headed. Then she would sit by me and talk with me and stroke my hair. A tingling came and took over my whole body and my vision wavered. Just as I felt I might lose consciousness, a crack sounded against the window as a rock hit it.

Dena jumped at the sound. She had been holding my hand and blotting my forehead with a cold cloth. I squeezed her hand and smiled weakly. I was pulled back to myself. "That is Robert, Dena. He is here, thank God in heaven. I need him here, Dena. You must sneak him up here. Go now."

Dena's eyes looked startled and concerned. "But, my lady…"

"Go now, Dena." I cried out as a pain felt as if were to rip my body in half. "Go!" I commanded. I knew I was leaving the woman an impossible task. How was she to get Robert past the guard? "Just bring him up here, and if the guards chase you, make sure you get all the way to my side before they stop. I will take care of them." I eeked out the words, and then pulled the light to me.

That is exactly how it happened. Not ten minutes later, Dena and Robert banged open the door to my outer room with the guards on their heels. I silently flung light at them, willing them away with all haste as yet another pain took my breath away. They complied; their minds completely bulled over by the power I exerted in my agony.

Dena glanced behind her at the strange behavior of the guards and began to ask a question. I stopped her by saying, "Thank you, Dena." My gaze left my maid to find Robert.

His beautiful blue eyes were ice until he took my face in his hands.

"Cutting it a little close, my love," I chided him as I pulled his outercoat, and thus him, toward me.

With his face an inch away, he whispered, "Dena told me it was time."

"Yes." I grunted as my body tightened and pain overwhelmed my insides.

Robert kissed my hair.

When the pain eased, I said, "you smell of horse," and with those words, my lunch and dinner rose up in my throat.

Dena must have recognized my green face for what it was, and quick as a viper, had a bowl under my chin. I deposited every meal I had ever eaten in my life in that bowl, as Robert held my hair back.

When I was finished, Dena spoke. "Well, my lady, that's the last of it. You should be ready to push your child out at any moment." She wiped my brow.

I looked at her confused.

"The motion of vomiting forces the way open for the child."

"Really?" Robert asked. "How is that...?"

I could see Robert's inquisitive face. "No, no, no, Robert Dudley. This is not the time for you to satisfy... ouch." I proceeded to howl through a pain, and Dena was right, it was far more serious than those before it. Once it passed, I finished, "to satisfy your curiosity."

I felt something. It was warm and wet. I went very still and then I lifted up the blanket. "Dena..." I sang in a terrified voice.

She looked and smiled. "It's not to be afraid of, my Lady, that there is your water." She turned to Robert. "Shoo, shoo. Get out of the way, man. It's time for your child to come into the world. You must leave."

Robert looked at me then. I saw what he was thinking. He knew how scared I was, he knew that birthing was the stuff of nightmares for me, and so he squeezed my hand and climbed onto the bed with me. Wrapping his arm around my shoulder, he said, "I will not leave. Here, my darling, lean on me. Let me help you."

"This is not the way it is done. You are not to be in here," Dena said almost pleadingly.

Robert's voice went cold. "I will not leave her," he said slowly.

"But, it's improper! You cannot see her; and when the time is here, I cannot hide her."

Even as another pain took me, I whispered, "remember Dena, he is the baby's father, he has seen it all before. Let him stay, he comforts me."

That quieted her down and before long, it was time to push.

Robert and I occupied the only two chairs in my bed chamber as we stared in amazement at our daughter. The tiny beautiful girl snuggled in my arms smacked her lips expectantly. Then she yawned grandly. Robert smiled, but did not take his eyes off our daughter as I looked over at him. I shivered a little as I thought of the pain and work that had brought this small child into the world. I would not forget how it all felt, how horrid it was; however, I would also never forget the look in Robert's eyes right now, and the feel of our precious beautiful infant next to me. The insides of her hands were so soft, and her little gums were so smooth, and the little hairs on her ears and shoulders made me smile. She was perfect. Her head was full of dark black hair and it smelled wonderful, like new skin.

Robert was looking at me now. His hand caressed my face and his eyes told me how he loved me and our daughter. "What shall we name her?"

I had given great thought to this. "I want to name her Anne."

He obviously had thought about it too, for he said, "I thought you might. It's perfect."

I snuggled the infant into my neck, and she latched onto me there and began to make a sweet sucking sound.

"Dianne, I believe it is time to feed her again," I called out, and the homely young woman Robert had brought with him to be Anne's wet-nurse came in and took my daughter from me. She was a gentle and kind soul. Her tale was one of sorrow and loss and desperation. Which made her perfect for the job we had for her.

Yet...

I had the strange urge to nurse my daughter myself. I knew that was not how things were done, nor could I keep it up since she would eventually be leaving with Robert and then I would be in terrible pain. 'If you begin the job of nursing, you best be prepared to finish it,' Dena had told me, and I knew I could not finish it.

So, I felt a bit of jealous resentment as I watched Dianne walk away with my child.

I attempted to push it down.

My husband must have seen all I felt on my face, for when I turned to him, I found him staring at me with such a look of sorrow. We shared a moment in which love for the man burned me so deeply, tears flooded my eyes.

I reached for his face and he leaned toward me to make it easier and our lips met. The happiness I felt and the love for the family we'd created overwhelmed me.

Days passed. It did not take long for Robert to become restless. I had to keep him in my rooms almost every moment, and anytime my jailer, Sir Bedingfield, would visit me—he feigned worry for my health, which seemed odd, for in the past, I had wondered if he were an enemy—I had to hide all trace of Robert, the child, and Dianne from his sight. It was quite exhausting.

Robert did leave the room at midnight and go for a ride, but beyond that, he was stuck with a bunch of women and a baby, day in and day out. I captured his attention in many ways: chess, conversation, books, kisses, and Anne. She was by far the best distraction. Still, Robert was a man of action. It only took him a few weeks to be stir-crazy.

I was about at my wit's end with Robert's moody pacing, when it was time for my appointment with the head of my house, as it was. Master Parry entered my rooms with his usual papers. Bills, the queen's wishes, news (that was allowed). Sir Bedingfield accompanied him, of course, to make sure all was up to the deprivation standards he insisted upon. It was a wonder that Sir Bedingfield allowed me to have servants.

Before, when I was pregnant and trying to hide the fact, I could abide his moods and cruel nature tolerably, but now, it rankled.

Master Parry knew what he was about, though, for he'd been doing it for years, so he discussed it all with placidity and I listened likewise. Until the end, where he dropped a cannon ball.

"My lady," he started carefully. "I know this is outside our usual..." That was as far as he got before Bedingfield broke in.

"No, no, Master Parry. She is a prisoner and not privy to outside interference or information."

Master Parry's feathers got ruffled at that. "My good sir," he all but shouted, "You have known me for a year almost and I have not even attempted to go outside your rules, and if it were not a direct request from the king, I would not dream of asking..."

That shut him up. But only for a moment. "The king? I have heard nothing from the king?"

"Well, you are not as well informed as you think then, not with the King nor with Elizabeth."

These words must have chastened him or perhaps got his curiosity up. Whatever the reason, when Master Parry continued with, "may I..."

The rather evil little man looked skeptically down his long slider nose at Master Parry and acquiesced, "very well."

"Thank you." He turned to me then, "My lady Princess, the king is very concerned about his friend and yours, Robert Dudley. No one can seem to find the fellow. It occurred to me that because you know him well, you might be able to shed light on his favorite hideaways? Information of that kind would be helpful, and might earn a return of favor." His eyebrows rose to indicate I should know I needed help getting out of this place. What none knew was that I did not want to get out of here. Not yet.

I kept my face straight as I pretended to consider. In truth, Robert was with Anne right through the doors to my sleeping chamber. He would know now that he was wanted and must go. And with him, he would take my less-than-a-month-old daughter.

After a moment, I shook my head and said, "I am sorry, Master

Parry. I wish I could help."

He sighed. "Ah, well. It was worth a try. But, if you should think of anything, send Dena."

"I will." I straightened my dress. "And speaking of which, Master Parry, Dena's family has been struggling. I was hoping you could give them a very nice sum so that they get through the winter." Of course, this was just a gift to her for helping me with the baby.

"I had not heard she was in need. Of course. Where do you want the funds to come from?"

"You flatter me, for you know as well as I that in my current predicament the moneys all come from the same source: Mary. Still, I trust you to do the right thing." I smiled at him. "Well, gentlemen, is that all?"

Master Parry rose. "Until next week, my lady." Bedingfield followed and they bowed their way out.

I knotted my hands up. A forbidding settling in my gut, for I knew with this news, Robert must go, and with him, Anne. Robert was the only one who could take her, and who knew when Mary would release me or when Robert could return? Robert's fate was still tenuous, and intricately mingled with the good pleasure of Phillip. If Mary had her way, she would stuff Robert back in the Tower faster than you could say "Machiavelli." This problem warranted a long discussion.

Robert's face held desperate emotion as he moved to me, kneeling by my side. "Oh Robert!" I wailed, "I love you so much... and Anne." I shook with the power of my despair. "This separation is going to tear me apart."

Robert took my face carefully in his hands, "My love, do not think of it that way. You, with this sacrifice, are saving her life and ours. In my home, as a motherless bastard child of mine, she will be cared for, provided for, and loved. I will keep her with me in my travels, always. Dena and Dianne, both very loyal women, will care for her, and when you are free, we will be together."

"But what of Amy?" I choked out the word. "Will she not hate Anne?"

"I have no intention of spending any time at all with Amy, though she is very motherly. If you recall, she took care of me for all that time after the rebellion. Still, I will not be leaving my bastard child with Amy. That would be a torture to her and, though my fealty and heart belong to you, I cannot torture another creature needlessly." He kissed me softly on the forehead. "Besides, I am a selfish man. Anne will be the piece of you I get to take with me."

I sobbed even harder. "But what of my piece of you? Why must I make all the sacrifices? Robert, it is more than I can bear!" He pulled me carefully from the chair, for I was still very sore from the birth, and into his lap on the floor. Raining kisses in my hair and tear-streaked face, he held me so tightly and pressed his lips so firmly into me, that it almost hurt, but I would not have asked him to stop if each kiss drew blood.

"I know you have done all the work, my love. I know that you have suffered in body, mind, and spirit. I know, I know." His kisses paused. "But perhaps you could try to think of it as my turn. My turn to sacrifice something. It has not been all bad. All those months Anne was inside of you, you were with her... feeling her move, loving her, talking to her. Now it is my turn to have that, and my chance to do something honorable. Do not begrudge me my chance." He wiped the tears from my face. "I get to protect her from the world, and sacrifice much: my freedom, my reputation and famed morals—for all will persecute me for having a bastard child. Amy will suffer the embarrassment of this also, and no doubt punish me for it. And who knows what Phillip and Mary will think or do? Yet with all of that, I get to do it for you... for Anne."

I looked up at him, my eyes asking unspoken questions. Sniffing, I said, "you are right. You have given me so many chances to change these circumstances, but I have continued to choose this. To choose us. And this choice... I... well, you and I, we made this choice together. We knew it would not be easy. It seems nothing that is worthwhile is easy."

Robert once again took my face in his hands. His passion charged the entire room as he said, "you are the strongest, most dedicated person I know. I could never love anyone as deeply as I love you. I will be on your side and by your side as long as you want me there. I swear it. As for this current predicament, I will do whatever you tell me to do, Elizabeth, for as much as Anne is mine, she is doubly yours. Whatever manly explanations I might make, I know better than to think you unable to handle a potentially deadly situation. So tell me what to do. I am yours to command." By the end of this fair and just speech, he was whispering.

When the time came for Robert and Anne to leave, we all wept. I kissed Robert's cheek gently and took in a deep breath of him as I said, "I hope you can see me again soon, Robert. I will be so forlorn without the two of you. Lord bless you both. Make a place for yourself in London, my love, for once I am set free, having you in London will make our situation much more livable." I would be brave. My voice was steady, at least.

With a touch to Anne's cheek, I turned reluctantly from them and looked at the two women sitting on the other side of the carriage. Filling myself with light, I said, "Dorothy, Dianne, from this moment forward you will never speak the name Elizabeth again. You will not know me or recall any of the circumstances that have happened here. It does not matter who asks you or who presses you, you will not be able to say or remember the circumstances of Anne's birth or your time here in Woodstock. Furthermore, you will watch Anne at all possible times and protect her as best you can. And you will loyally serve Sir Robert until he releases you." I sent the light to them and then turned to my husband. "That should cover everything." I said with a sniff.

"Indeed, it will," Robert replied and looked at me with admiration. "I love you." Then with one last knowing smile for Robert and a kiss for Anne, I closed the carriage door and told the driver to be on his way.

As I watched them drive away, I felt that I had never been so imprisoned in my life, and, God forgive me, but I hated my sister for it.

February 1555
Woodstock, Oxfordshire

After several days of crying in my rooms, my dreary life pressed on, as impossible as it seemed. Master Parry himself came to the castle under some pretense and spoke to Dena—who had taken up the job as my maid—in a hushed and private way before Sir Henry arrived to bustle him away.

Fortunately, he'd had enough time to deliver the dire news.

"My lady, Bishop John Hooper, John Rogers, and John Cardmaster were arrested two weeks ago. They were warned, but they refused to cease their heretical activities. So the council put them on trial." Dena was dry-washing her hands and her voice was shaking. "My lady, all three were condemned two days ago, and Master Parry comes to tell us that they are burnt. I daren't continue, my lady, but that is not all; there have been many other gentry folk burned."

"God have mercy on us all!" I said and fell to my knees, as that prayer was in my heart as well as on my lips. "Have any recanted amid the flames?"

"None my lady, but Master Parry says that the mood of the people has hardened and that they are not pleased with their queen. Moreover, my lady, it has enraged those openly Protestant to call themselves martyrs, and act as a bravado in facing their accusers."

"I knew it would. All one must do to cause a whole slew of brava-dos is kill someone in the name of religion."

Later, I heard that many were calling for me to do something about the burnings, which were growing in number each week; and each week, many Protestants left the country for their own safety. There was nothing that I could do. Mary and Philip were only hurting their cause by kill-ing off Englishmen and scaring them off English soil. Who would fight France if all loyal to England were forced to flee?

March 1555
Woodstock, Oxfordshire

My life was misery. I had not heard from Robert. With all the blood being spilt by my sister, Sir Henry tightened my freedoms, and, for the first time, I agreed with him—though a letter from my husband would have eased my mind so much, for I had no idea if he had succeeded in wooing the king and queen. Sir Henry did not want heretics to get a hold of me, or for any ideas of escape amidst the upheaval to be formed. My life was truly in constant danger, from many sides. Those who wanted me to save them and those who supported Mary's righteous, yet gory, purge.

That was not all.

For months, I had a dreamt of Mary. Over and over, I saw blood dripping from her signet ring-encircled finger. I thought it was my death this dream foretold, but now it seemed otherwise. Perhaps the dream meant this horrid English re-baptism to Catholicism, not by fire, as the apostles stated, but by blood. The problem was, I did not know if my blood was included in the foretelling. Alone, petrified, and threatened, my life was a misery.

Spring was at hand and still, I could do nothing but wait and sulk. I had nothing to employ my mind with, except the fear that the next person brought to the stake would be me, or worse, Robert.

Despite my worry, I found myself more and more resigned to my situation.

The idea that Mary had broken me with all this imprisonment sent me to my bed for many weeks. I had always prided myself in being somewhat like a stallion, yet here I was: abed. Cold. Hopeless.

It was so cold all the time.

April 1555
Woodstock, Oxfordshire

I wondered what Robert was doing. How could he forsake me for so long? And what of Anne?

There were whispers that Mary's spirits were up, which gave me false hope, for it was April and there was no word of my release or change in my circumstance. At present, I was not sure I wanted to be released. For Mary knew, or suspected, my sentiments, and what better martyr to the Catholic cause than me, the daughter of two heretics and—at present—her very own replacement to the throne? Of course, she would wait to act after she had her child and all the traditions were seen to. The people would be mollified by a new child prince, so she could do away with me without hindrance.

Not two days later, I received a message from Master Parry that it was time for Mary to enter her confinement, but she hadn't yet. Questions were being asked.

Dena analyzed the report with me after Master Parry left. Sir Henry could not stop my maid from talking to me, not while she dressed me.

"The queen celebrated Easter at Hampton and showed herself to a large crowd, where all admired her swollen belly. Though it was not quite so swollen as it ought."

"I wonder what it all could mean. Where does this doubt come from? Of course she is with child and she is close to giving birth." However, before I could completely adjust my mind to the news, Sir Henry knocked impatiently at my door, and was entering my chamber a few minutes later in what looked like a jolly manner.

"Your highness, your highness, you will not believe the news I just received." I had never seen him in this happy mood before. Not even during the small festivities that we had enjoyed at Christmas.

"What is it, sir?"

"The queen summons you to court," he said with delight in his face.

I felt blood drain from my face, and I turned to Dena, my hands instantly shaking. She gripped them hard, her eyes serious. She waited for my reaction. I was waiting, too. It was so unexpected and sudden. No hints or rumors that she was warming to me. No foreplay of letters testing the water. No whispers. Just a summons. I considered what this might mean.

She obviously did not want people to know she summoned me, which did not bode well for my prospects. If she meant me no harm, would she not just invite me openly?

Sir Henry cut off my thoughts with, "we are to hurry and make no unnecessary stops along the way."

This confirmed my suspicions. This was a clandestine deal.

I could not think of anything else to say, so I asked, "are you certain?"

"Yes, my lady, I have the letter here." He fluttered the papers before my nose but did not let me touch them.

I did see it was in Mary's own hand, though I could not read it. "Who brought this letter?"

"Really, my lady…"

But with his air and tone, I knew exactly what he was going to say. I cut him off.

"Sir Henry. It seems I am a prisoner no longer." I put on a smile as best I could and, asserting my dominance over him, stood straight and waited for his reply.

"Well, if you must know, it was Sir Robert Tyrwhitt."

The name struck pain and fear into my heart. Both of my captors in the same house. It seemed my shame and punishment had come full circle.

This told me something else. Sir Robert knew how to keep things to himself. Mary knew this. It must be why she asked him to deliver the tidings. She did not want any to know she summoned me to court. For the people would stop her if they thought she might harm me. So, it was to be done in secret. Would she burn me a heretic as she had so many others? Would she behead me as a sick twist of ironic vengeance? Would she put me on trial again?

I bit my lip, my hands shaking once more, and my only thought, a question: was this my end?

La fin